Adam moved his hand, nudging her chin up with his fist. And then he kissed her.

He took advantage of her submission to part her lips with his tongue and sweep inside, taking her sharp gasp of cooler night air and replacing it with raw heat. In a mist of sensuality, Roane was only vaguely aware of him wrapping his arm around her waist and tugging her closer to the edge of her chair. Her arms lifted, hands sliding around the column of his neck to hold him tight as their knees bumped together. Every doubt, every fear, every voice of reason in her head short-circuited except one.

Why haven't I been kissed like this before?

We can't help but love a bad boy!

The wicked glint in his eye…the rebellious streak
that's a mile wide. His untamed unpredictability.
The way he'll always get what he wants, on his
own terms. The sheer confidence, charisma and
barefaced charm of the guy.…

In this brand-new miniseries from Harlequin
Presents, these heroes have all that—
and a lot more besides!
They're

Wild, Wealthy and Wickedly Sexy!

Don't miss it—because in these hot new stories,
bad is definitely better!

Trish Wylie

ONE NIGHT WITH THE REBEL BILLIONAIRE

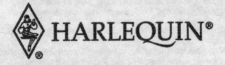

TORONTO • NEW YORK • LONDON
AMSTERDAM • PARIS • SYDNEY • HAMBURG
STOCKHOLM • ATHENS • TOKYO • MILAN • MADRID
PRAGUE • WARSAW • BUDAPEST • AUCKLAND

Recycling programs
for this product may
not exist in your area.

ISBN-13: 978-0-373-12833-4

ONE NIGHT WITH THE REBEL BILLIONAIRE

First North American Publication 2009.

Copyright © 2009 by Trish Wylie.

Printed in U.S.A.

All about the author...
Trish Wylie

TRISH WYLIE tried various careers before
getting the one she'd wanted since her late teens.
She flicked her blond hair over her shoulder
while playing the promotions game, patted her
manicured hands on the backs of musicians while
working in the music business, smiled sweetly at
awkward customers during the retail nightmare
known as the run-up to Christmas, and has gotten
completely lost in her car in every single town in
Ireland while working as a sales rep. And it took
all that character-building and a healthy sense of
humor to get her dream job, which lets her spend
her days in reindeer slippers, with her hair in
whatever band she can find to keep it out of the
way and makeup as vague and distant a memory as
manicured nails. She's happy she gets to create the
kind of dream man she'd still like to believe is out
there somewhere. If it turns out he is, she promises
she'll let you know...after she's been out for a new
wardrobe, a manicure and a makeover....

For Sharon W—friend, reader and
fellow admirer of hot and gorgeous horses.
Luv ya, babes!

CHAPTER ONE

'EXCUSE ME. I'M SORRY. This is a private beach.'

Roane Elliott stepped tentatively closer. A full moon lit everything around her in shades of silver and grey, with black shadows that seemed to breathe with the ebb and flow of the tide. But her surroundings didn't worry her as much as the presence of the stranger; she might have known every rock, every path, every place the sand sank deeper beneath her feet—but she also knew she was too far away from a 911 call for it to help if she got into trouble…

Her footsteps faltered. But it wasn't the sudden 911 thought that had done it; it was because she was now standing close enough to see he was—

Her eyes widened. Oh, dear Lord. *He was naked!*

More than that, he was an Adonis. In the silvery light every tight muscle was defined in shadowy dips and shimmering planes from wide shoulders to tapering waist to taut… Her mouth went dry.

He turned around, so Roane swiftly averted her gaze, and mumbled under her breath, *'Look at his face.'*

When she glanced at him from the corner of her eye her errant gaze didn't do what it was told. Well, who could blame her? He was sensational. She damped her lips as if she could taste him on the air before forcing her gaze sharply upwards, her palms itching with an almost primal urge to reach out and *touch*.

'This is a private beach,' she repeated with a little more force, lifting her chin to make her point. 'You shouldn't be here.'

'The ocean belongs to everyone.' Even the tone of his voice was magical.

Well, he could take that deep, rumbling, deliciously masculine voice of his that was doing something completely undiscovered to her pulse rate and—

Her thought process stalled. Wow, he had the most amazing muscle definition on his chest and upper arms. Not pumped up, steroid induced definition, oh, no. He looked like the kind of man who worked at something very physical for a living. Or was a natural sportsman of some kind, a swimmer maybe—no, not lean enough for a swimmer. Not that he was fat anywhere she could see, which was pretty much everywhere if she chose to take a good long look. And she could have, because he wasn't the least bit embarrassed about being naked—in fact, he placed his hands on his hips, almost daring her to go right ahead and look.

Thankfully the silent arrogance brought her gaze north to his shadowed face rather than travelling south, which, deep down, it *really* wanted to do…

She cleared her throat. 'You're not in the ocean; you're standing on the beach. And it's *private*. You have to go. There are security patrols.'

It was a lie. But he didn't know that.

In the shadows the suggestion of a crooked smile appeared, 'Your beach, is it?'

'It belongs to the family I work for. I—' She'd been about

to tell him she had a place a few hundred yards away. No doubt she'd be casually discussing the weather with him next. 'I have permission to be here.'

When he took a step forwards she instinctively stepped back. 'I know self-defence, so don't try anything. I'm a black belt in ju-kwando.'

A brief chuckle of deep laughter preceded the dropping of his hands and another forward step. 'My clothes are behind you. And for future reference it's ju-jitsu or tae kwon do. Nice try. But I won't bite you.'

Roane moved to the side as he stepped closer, colour rising on her cheeks when he inclined his head and added a low, 'Not unless you ask me to.'

She opened her mouth to say something cutting in return and couldn't seem to get her brain to work well enough to form a sentence. But she liked to think any red-blooded female would have been the same when confronted with such temptation. He was one of those men that would take what he wanted when he wanted, wasn't he? She could *feel it.* There was just something very erotic about that—in the darkness—when he was naked… For a girl as inexperienced as Roane it was quite the realization. But what kind of woman was turned on by a naked stranger in the middle of the night? She tried to think of a reason why she was still standing there.

Making sure he leaves, she told herself.

Liar, an inner voice replied.

The rasp of a zipper invited her to glance back at him. His elbows bent as his hands worked on the belt of his jeans, he asked, 'You live here?'

'Answering that would hardly be a good move on my part, now would it?'

'I'd say you left the region of good moves when you approached a stranger to begin with, wouldn't you?'

When he turned his face towards the ocean the moon lit his face. For a brief moment Roane was struck by how *beautiful* he was. Not a word normally used to describe men, she knew, but he was. There was no way to tell what colour his hair or eyes were in the restricted light, but she had a sneaking suspicion they'd merely be icing on the cake.

His face had a symmetry to it that she'd never seen before—almost as if he'd been artificially created. Twinned dark pools that suggested large deep-set eyes, a perfectly straight nose, a mouth—dear heaven, that mouth; full lips practically calling out to be kissed. He even had a square jaw.

Roane was just the teensiest bit smitten.

He looked at her and smiled the most sinfully sexy smile. Because he knew, didn't he? Looking the way he did, how could he fail to know women were smitten by him? Judging by the beast of a motorcycle she'd discovered parked at the top of the wooden walkway down to the beach she'd bet he drove all over the country leaving trails of smitten women behind him. There was an addictive sense of—freedom—to him too; as if he belonged where he stood and nowhere else. Nothing would stop him from going where he wanted when he wanted, from swimming naked on a private beach or seducing a woman in the moonlight…

He could reach out and haul her to him, press those practised lips to hers, lower her to the soft sand beneath their feet, surround her body with his and—

Erotic images flashed across her brain, her body aching low inside at the very thought of that kind of an encounter. Just once in her life. She could almost hear the ragged breathing; feel the sweat-slickened skin…

Roane choked out the words, 'Please leave.'

His answer was slow, voice so husky she felt her breasts grow heavy in response. 'Scared, little girl?'

Roane frowned at the words. Why did they sound familiar? She didn't know who he was, but a part of her suddenly felt she should recognize him. 'Do I know you?'

'No one here knows me.'

When he turned and bent over to retrieve the rest of his belongings a shadow tracked the line of his spine, disappearing into the slight gape at the back of his jeans. The muscles in his shoulders worked as he moved, large hands reaching out and casually lifting what looked like a shirt and a jacket and boots. No underwear, she noted. And then he was turning to face her again, tucking the items casually against his hips.

'Taking a chance approaching a naked stranger on a beach in the dark, you know that, don't you, little girl?'

Why did he keep calling her that? Okay, so compared to him she *was* little. He had to be six feet two easy; Roane was five feet five. And beside all that defined muscle and inherent strength she was positively sylph-like in comparison. But being called a little girl at the age of twenty-seven should surely have felt patronizing to her. Instead it felt distinctly…sexual…and Roane was certain he knew that.

'I told you, there'll be a security—'

'No, there won't.'

She felt a flicker of panic. 'You don't know that.'

'Yes—' he continued looking at her '—I do.'

Who *was* this guy? The end of Martha's Vineyard they were on wasn't known for a large influx of motorcycle-riding bad boys. Frankly, anyone unfamiliar with the island would never have found the beach to begin with. But the main house on the bluff was certainly rich pickings for thieves. Maybe he'd been checking out the Bryant place? Was that it? Had he been filling in time on the beach while he waited for everyone to go to bed?

Roane had always had a very active imagination.

The stranger moved his clothes to the same hand as his boots, before reaching out to her. When she flinched back from it his low voice sounded irritated. 'I won't hurt you.'

'I don't know that.'

'You're still stood there so you must feel it or self-preservation would have kicked in.' He beckoned with long fingers. 'Come here.'

'Why?'

'I want to see you.'

'Why?'

Sighing impatiently, he stepped forwards and lifted her chin with the crook of his forefinger, turning her face to the light while she looked sideways at him with wide eyes. She didn't move—she couldn't seem to find the strength to move. It was surreal.

Trapping her chin between his thumb and forefinger he angled his head and examined her face at a maddeningly leisurely pace; thumb smoothing back and forth almost absentmindedly. Then he let go—leaving the heated brand of his touch against her skin.

'Grew up some, didn't you, little girl?'

Roane blinked at him as he turned away, her feet carrying her forwards as he stepped silently onto the end of the wooden walkway. 'Who are you?'

He didn't look back, his deep voice carrying on the night air. 'Night, Roane.'

* * *

'Hey, Jake?'

Roane jogged across to her friend's side when she spotted him on the laneway between the main house and the guest quarters the next morning. 'Wait up.'

He turned, a broad smile in place when he spotted her. 'Morning, sunshine.'

'Morning.' She couldn't resist stopping for a similar smile in return before falling into step beside him. They'd been friends since they'd been in nappies. And whereas most women were immediately struck by his tall, dark and handsome good looks Roane had long since outgrown the stage of being anywhere in the region of starry eyed. He was like a brother to her.

'Do you have a visitor on the estate? There was someone on the beach on my way home last night.'

Jake lifted dark brows. 'Was there?'

'Yeah—it was the weirdest thing.' She pushed her hands into the pockets of her jeans and skipped over the bigger details, like naked male glory and a soul-deep feminine reaction to that nakedness. There were some things a gal just didn't discuss with a brother. 'He seemed to know me.'

Jake's chin jerked up a little, his gaze on the guest house. 'Did he? Well, then—let's just see if it's who I think it was, shall we?'

Roane frowned in confusion as Jake slung a long arm over her shoulders and tugged her close to whisper conspiratorially in her ear, 'We *do* have a visitor…'

Roane kept her hands in her pockets and allowed Jake to steer her up the grassy path and through the open doors of the house that her own home could have fitted inside at least a dozen times. Guests at the Bryant estate were treated to the kind of luxury most folks would be hard-pressed to find in a five star hotel.

Exquisite views over the ocean from the custom-built, architect-designed house were the first treat. The fact it was nestled in fifteen-odd acres of mature trees and established gardens overlooking a private cove was the next. Then add ten thousand square feet of house with five bedrooms, gourmet kitchen and countless luxury amenities, including master suite with Jacuzzi and great room with cathedral ceilings and two-storey stone fireplace and, *well...*

Modern-day European royalty probably lived in less.

'Hello?' Jake released her as they stepped through into the beechwood kitchen, bright light streaming in through the many windows to bathe the room in golden warmth. 'Anyone home?'

He stopped so suddenly Roane almost walked into the wall of his back. Frowning, she stepped around him, ready to make a comment about a little warning being a good thing when her jaw dropped.

Her mystery man gave her a cursory glance before turning his attention to Jake. 'Coffee?'

'Yeah, please.'

He turned and poured two cups while Roane continued to gape. She'd been right about the hair and eye colour being icing. In fact if anything he was even more stunning in sunlight than he was in moonlight. She now knew his cropped hair was dark blond, the bright light in the room picking up lighter strands in the spikes that looked as if they'd been formed by long fingers raked casually from front to back. As for his eyes...well, she might have to be a little closer to be sure, but they looked pretty good to her...

Jake was talking again. "Found the key, then?"

'Looks like it.' He turned and placed a mug into each of

their hands without asking Roane if she wanted anything. 'Add what you need—it's all on the counter.'

Then he caught her gaze for a moment, a knowing light sparkling in the stunning green-flecked brown of his eyes. 'Morning, Roane.'

Suddenly she knew who he was. *'Adam?'*

While Jake moved over to the kitchen table Adam smiled lazily, lowering his head to whisper, *'Now* she remembers me.'

Before Roane could say anything in reply, he turned away and slid onto the curved bench facing his brother. 'The detective agency was a bit much, don't you think?'

Jake shrugged. 'It wasn't like you sent Christmas cards every year so we'd know how to reach you.'

'And there was possibly a reason for that…'

Jake pursed his lips as Roane slid onto the bench beside him, immediately feeling the need to ease the tension by teasing him. 'You hired a detective agency to find him? You didn't mention that. Was he a raincoat-wearing private-eye type?'

Jake smiled. 'No; I was disappointed actually.'

'If you'd told me we could have searched for one. It would have been much more fun.' She smiled back at him. But a part of her was hurt he hadn't told her he was searching for Adam. It was a huge deal. She could remember a time in their lives when they'd talked about everything and anything.

When she glanced across the table she found the prodigal Bryant lounging casually, one long arm slung along the back of the wooden bench while sunshine glowed off the deep tan on his skin. But the nonchalance was a façade, wasn't it? Roane could *feel* the intensity in him while his impossibly thick lashes flickered as he studied the interaction across the table.

His gaze crashed into hers for the space of two heartbeats and Roane felt her breath hitch. How did he *do* that with just a look?

He turned his attention to Jake. 'How bad is he?'

'He has good days and bad.' Jake leaned forwards, cupping his mug between his hands and idly turning it while he spoke. 'We try to keep him to a routine; that helps.'

Roane's voice softened. 'He'll be glad to see you.'

Adam glanced briefly at her again, then back to Jake. 'Lucid?'

'Short-term memory loss initially—confused some days; angry, prone to mood swings—'

Adam's mouth twisted wryly as he turned his profile to them and looked outside. 'Not much change, then…'

Jake didn't smile. 'Still Dad, yes. But it's only a matter of time before we're looking at language breakdown, long term memory loss and a general withdrawal as his senses decline. Once diagnosed they give them an average life expectancy of seven years. And they diagnosed him two years ago. So if you want to make your peace you'd best make it now.'

Roane frowned when Adam didn't respond. Surely he wouldn't have come home if he hadn't intended to make his peace with his father before it was too late? She knew very little about why he'd left, but then Adam had been an enigma long before that. When he'd left she had barely been fifteen, Jake a year older—and they'd been thick as thieves. But the rebellious Adam had been twenty-one. Six years wasn't that big a gap for adults, but back then it had seemed like a lot more. Adam had been a young man, and a deeply unhappy one at that. He hadn't wanted to spend time hanging round with two carefree teenagers during their endless halcyon summers.

Jake pushed again. 'If you want to look the business over before you make any decisions, then—'

'There's a hurry, is there?'

God, he was so *cold!* Roane felt a chill run down her spine, fighting the need to shiver at his reaction while he calmly lifted his mug to his mouth. If he didn't give a damn why had he come home at all? Why not stay as lost to his family as he'd been for the last twelve years?

'Yes,' Jake informed him.

Roane blinked at her friend. What was going on?

Adam apparently knew. 'Gonna buy me out, are you?'

'If I have to.' Jake nodded once.

Roane leaned her elbow on the arm of the wooden bench and rested her forefinger along the side of her face, hiding her mouth behind the rest of her fingers. Adam Bryant might be pretty amazing to look at, but he wasn't much of a personality, was he? Didn't he feel the least bit guilty that he'd left everything on his younger brother's shoulders? She might not know much, but she knew Jake had been tense of late, preoccupied, *older* somehow... Running the Bryant empire alone had been taking its toll.

As if he could sense her disapproval, Adam's gaze flickered briefly towards her again, then back to Jake just as fast. Frankly it was starting to bug Roane. It felt as if he was dismissing her presence—as if he didn't feel she should even be there. But if Jake thought that he wouldn't have brought her in with him, would he? With the benefit of hindsight, she knew he'd probably felt the need for moral support.

'I'll take a look at the figures,' Adam told Jake.

'There's a board meeting at three in Manhattan. Roane can fly you in, can't you, Ro?'

Did she have to? She smiled. ''Course I can.'

Adam didn't look at her. 'I'll drive.'

'It's at least five and a half hours by road—you'd need to leave in an hour,' Roane pointed out. 'It's less than two hours by air; you wouldn't have to leave til noon. I'm sure you'll want to spend time with your dad before you go…'

When he looked at her again she quirked her brows. Not that it had any effect on him. Instead he held her gaze steadily, as if to prove he could having spent so little time looking her directly in the eye.

'You fly?'

'Yes.' Silently she willed him to make a comment about it being a step up from the chauffeur-cum-handyman position her father had held for most of his life.

He didn't. Instead he took a deep breath that expanded the material of his dark green T-shirt while his gaze shifted back to Jake. 'When's the next board meeting?'

'Two weeks.'

'Right.' Adam looked out the windows, his jaw tensing while he thought, eyes narrowed against the bright light. Then he nodded briefly. 'Fine. I'll fly.'

Roane lowered her hand and looked at Jake. 'I'll book the slot. You coming?'

'No, I'll go ahead. I already have a slot.'

Which meant she got to fly down with Adam on her own. Fantastic. That should make for a chatty flight. Roane couldn't remember ever spending time in close proximity to someone she found so intensely physically attractive yet didn't like at the same time.

Jake nudged her to indicate he wanted to slide out. 'I'll take Adam over to the house.'

'I remember the way.'

Roane pursed her lips at Adam's reply as she slid off the

bench and walked to the sink to toss her untouched coffee away, Jake's voice calm behind her.

'I'm going over anyway.'

When he joined her at the sink she looked up at him, mouthing a concerned You okay?

He winked and mouthed back, Fine.

Automatically she took his mug and rinsed it out after she'd done her own, adding a plate and a couple of pieces of cultery that were lying on the side too and not noticing Jake had moved away until she turned—and walked straight into the solid wall of Adam's chest. One large hand shot up to grasp her elbow as she staggered back, her spine bumping the edge of the counter as she looked down at his hand with wide eyes.

Because it was like being touched by a live wire.

A spark of electricity shot up her arm, under her skin and into her veins where it picked up speed with the rapid beat of her heart. The tingling then radiated outwards, licking over her bare shoulder and down over her chest where her nipples beaded into tight buds against the lace of her bra.

Adam let go so suddenly her gaze shot upwards.

When his eyes narrowed an almost imperceptible amount Roane blinked at him. He'd felt that? What in the name of heaven *was that* anyway? It couldn't even be put down to static electricity—not when it was bare skin touching bare skin. Could it? Science had never been her thing, after all.

'Ro? You coming?' Jake's familiar voice sounded from the open doorway.

'Mmm-hmm, yeah.' She frowned as she stepped around Adam, absent-mindedly rubbing where he had touched her as if to remove an invisible mark.

Adam took a half step in her direction so that her shoulder

brushed his upper arm, the rumble of his voice low and steeped with innuendo.

'Be seeing you. *Little girl.*'

She stopped and smiled sugary sweet. 'How long did you say you were staying?'

'I didn't.'

A quick glance at the doorway showed that Jake had already stepped outside. Suddenly Roane felt edgy without him there. Her hesitation didn't help either, because when she looked up at Adam it was in time to see he'd noticed the same thing.

'Finally caught him, did you?'

What? She gaped when she realized what he meant, 'I wasn't ever—' She frowned at the sudden need to defend herself. 'My relationship with Jake is none of your business.'

When she stepped away he reached out and grabbed her wrist, lifting her hand to study it. 'No ring.'

Roane tugged her arm. 'Let go.'

He held on. 'How come?'

Not that she had all that much experience with men, but Roane had never met such a Neanderthal. For goodness' sake, the man practically *grunted* a conversation!

She tugged again, harder this time, determined not to pay attention to the low thrumming of awareness in her abdomen. 'That's still none of your business.'

Adam repositioned his fingers, his gaze studying her wrist for a moment before he looked sideways at her and a smile began to play with the corners of his mouth. The way the green in his eyes had darkened, the way that half a smile was forming—it threw rational thought clean out of her head. Until she realized what he was smiling about…

He'd just felt her pulse jumping about in her wrist. He

knew what he was doing to her disobedient body. More than that—he was *pleased* about it! The arrogant great—

Adam let go.

So Roane did the mature thing and practically ran from the room. Let him go right ahead and think she was with Jake if he wanted to. It made her reaction to Adam even worse than it already was, but at least she wouldn't have to deal with it, because surely he wouldn't make a pass at his brother's girlfriend?

Cowardly, the voice said inside her head, using Jake as some kind of protective shield. But she ignored it. Caveman had never done it for her before, and it sure as heck wasn't starting to now.

Even if Adam Bryant looked like the kind of bad news every girl secretly dreamed of finding.

CHAPTER TWO

'MVY TOWER…MERIDIAN five eight nin-er two November ready to taxi with mike…right turnout southeast bound.'

Only when they were cruising at five and a half thousand feet did Roane truly experience all that she loved best about flying: serenity, control and exhilaration. All around them were blue skies, below them the mirrored aquamarine of the ocean. Things were so calm she could have switched to autopilot. But that would have left time for conversation with her passenger, and it was bad enough he'd got in the cockpit instead of sitting in back where she could have pretended he wasn't there. So she didn't.

Unable to resist, she glanced to her side and noticed long fingers tapping restlessly against the taut trouser-clad thigh that was moving to the rhythm of a bouncing heel. An errant smile immediately blossomed in her chest as the realization hit her.

'Not that good a flier, huh?'

When she bit down on her lower lip to control the smile Adam frowned. 'I'm good. *Thanks.*'

'Mmm-hmm.' She nodded, letting his sarcastic 'thanks' roll over her head. 'The tapping foot is a sure sign of relaxation.'

The tapping of his foot abruptly stopped, long fingers

curling into a fist. His knuckles were just white enough for Roane to suspect he was forcibly keeping his leg still. It was the first time since she'd met him on the beach that she'd felt she had the upper hand—it was empowering, especially considering every time she laid eyes on him her hormones seemed to go into overdrive. When he'd turned up at the airport she'd surreptitiously rolled her eyes at how good he looked in a dark suit. One glance at him and every part of her that had ever been attracted to intelligence and wit and congeniality went straight to hell. Apparently to be replaced with a cell-deep genetic need to mate with the strongest of the species for the sake of the human race...

But his reaction to being in the air meant her pilot's conscience insisted she make small talk to help take his mind off it. Sometimes Roane truly wished she had a meaner streak.

'Clear skies from here to New York; we won't even hit turbulence. Honest.'

'Right.'

Roane studied his tense profile, then took a breath and decided to throw caution to the wind and just say what she thought. 'You're not much of a talker, are you?'

Adam's reply was so low she mightn't have heard it if they weren't wearing mikes to go with the matching head sets. 'The secret of being boring is to say everything.'

Roane stared at him in amazement. He couldn't be serious. 'And where did we pick up *that* excuse?'

'Voltaire.'

Her brows lifted. 'Quote of the day?'

The vaguest hint of a smile appeared. 'No.'

Well, that went well. If Roane didn't know better she'd have said he was enigmatic on purpose. But before she could steer the conversation in a direction where she might glean some insight, Adam exhaled loudly and leaned back into his seat, his chin dropping as he studied the array of dials and readouts.

'Tell me how it works.'

He wanted a flying lesson? In Roane's experience it wasn't how people who were afraid of flying tended to react. Maybe he meant the theory of it? Okay—she could do the *basic* theory of it.

'One sec.' She engaged the autopilot and leaned back, turning and folding her arms across her breasts. 'It's flying itself now. But if the ground suddenly starts looking bigger, yell.'

'Funny,' Adam said dryly.

'Let's see.' Roane considered the ceiling for a moment, starting with something she'd read somewhere. 'Basically it all centres around Newton's idea that for every action, there is an equal and opposite reaction.'

Then she ad-libbed, warming to her subject, 'So you know when you let go of an inflated balloon and it flies all over the room? That's kinda like thrust in an airplane engine; it propels the plane into the air...' Unfolding an arm, she made a sweep with one hand to highlight the 'plane into the air' part; quite pleased with the analogy until she found him studying her with hooded eyes.

His deep voice held an edge of barely concealed disgust. 'When did you decide I was an idiot?'

Finding her mouth dry, Roane swallowed before coming back with a pathetically weak-voiced, 'Short Neanderthal grunted answers might possibly have done it.'

'I understand Newton's theories.'

A nervous bubble of laughter formed in her chest, but with effort she managed to keep her reaction to a teasing smile. 'Maybe you could explain them to me some time. I just keep the thing in the air. I've never felt the need to know the science that goes with it.'

She batted her lashes innocently.

'I'm sure to get your pilot's licence you had to be a step or two up from dumb blonde. How long have you been flying?'

'A long time—and I haven't killed anyone…' she paused for effect, shrugging one shoulder '…yet.'

The fleeting smile twitched the corner of his mouth; brown softening the green of his eyes. For a brief second, to Roane's astonishment, there was even a hint of deep laughter lines fanning out from the corners of his eyes, suggesting he laughed more often than she'd had evidence of so far. Leaving her wondering what it would take to make him laugh out loud—without holding back the way he was.

She *really* wanted to hear that sound.

But the fleeting smile was gone as fast as it arrived. When she studied him he studied her right back and then jerked his head in the direction of the controls. 'Run me through the basics.'

'Of actual flying rather than the theory of flight?'

'Yes.'

Roane sucked her bottom lip in and let it go with a slight 'pop', the words coming out before she could stop them. 'It's a control thing for you, isn't it?'

Adam blinked lazily, 'Could be.'

She couldn't really work him out, and it was disconcerting. But then it wasn't as if she were all that worldly-wise. She had met a fairly diverse selection of people in her time, but Adam? Adam was something new. Adam was *fascinating* to her if she were honest about it, which she wasn't about to be. At least not out loud.

She adjusted her mike, and when she spoke she heard the

distorted version of her own voice echoed louder in her ears. 'On the floor are pedals that operate the brakes and rudder. Push the right pedal, the rudder turns to the right. Push the left pedal, the rudder turns left. With me so far?'

Adam had dipped his chin and moved his knees apart so he could see the floor. But when she asked the question he glanced sideways, his tone still dry. 'I'll try and keep up.'

Roane smiled, turning away to check the readouts while she continued, 'The pilot controls the airplane by using a control wheel—the stick. This lets you move the elevators on the tail and the ailerons on the wings, which in turn move the airplane. Still with me?'

A deep sigh was magnified by the mike.

Still smiling, Roane shifted positions so she was leaning her upper body closer. 'Hands on the stick.'

Adam swiped his large palms across his thighs before lifting them and placing them tight on either side of the stick, his knuckles white. So with a roll of her eyes Roane couldn't seem to stop herself from asking, 'Jeez, Adam, would you grab hold of a woman like that?'

He shot her a sideways glare.

'Let me know when you want to find out.' He flexed his fingers and looked down at the controls. 'Keep going.'

The throwaway invitation sent a thrumming pulse of anticipation to the centre of her body, even though Roane knew instinctively it had been a knee-jerk reaction to her runaway tongue. 'Towards you the nose comes up—away the nose goes down. But I warn you, you touch the throttle at any point I may have to kill you myself before we hit the ground…'

He swallowed. 'And that's where exactly?'

Roane somehow managed not to laugh. She knew he wouldn't appreciate it, even if she did tell him her urge to giggle was partly because she was finding the chink in his armour so humanizing. Adam wasn't the kind of man who would like being told vulnerability was appealing, was he? So instead she reached for his large hands, her smaller ones nowhere near able to cover them as she curled her fingers around his.

'Between us.' She kept her gaze focused on their hands when he turned to look for the throttle, the heat of his skin beneath her cool fingers mesmerizing beyond belief to her. What would hands that size feel like on her body? Images immediately flickered through her brain in answer to the silent question, so that when she spoke her voice sounded embarrassingly breathless to her.

'There. That's it. A little forwards the nose drops…a little back…and…erm…'

She'd made the mistake of glancing up at him. When she found his face disconcertingly close to hers she faltered; his intense gaze focused on her mouth as she damped her lips. The man really did have the most ridiculously thick eyelashes.

'The—uh…the nose comes up…' She swallowed and forced air into her aching chest. Then his scent hit her. She'd been aware of it since they'd closed the cabin doors, but up close…up close and with the heat of his skin to magnify it. *Dear heaven…*

Roane was no expert, but she was a long-time fan of scented candles. There were notes of citrus in there, maybe blackcurrant…and then there was a hint of sandalwood, a suggestion of mulberry and just possibly a whisper of amber. It was the most *enticing* combination…

She breathed deep and practically sighed with contentment as she exhaled.

He was staring at her.

And he continued studying her with silent intensity, leaving Roane floundering. 'Okay, well, erm…left is left and right is right. Basically…'

The smile started in his eyes. 'Said that too…'

Well, how was she supposed to concentrate with him sitting as close as he was, looking the way he did and smelling as good as he was? Letting go of his hands, she sat back in her seat.

'Don't move the stick a minute.'

The change was so smooth it would have taken an expert to notice it. Then Roane was in control again. If Adam *was* seeking control by asking for the impromptu flying lesson, then she could understand that, she supposed. Having control of her plane again immediately made her feel better. He might be able to take possession of her body's reactions simply by breathing in and out. But by distracting herself with the everyday business of flying Roane could focus her mind elsewhere. She *could.*

'Just relax and feel my movements through the stick. That's it. Smoothly…'

Suddenly the control she had took on sexual undertones for her. She'd never been in a relationship with a man where she'd had the courage to be one of those women who took control. She'd never asked to be touched a particular way or in a certain place; nothing that might have made the experience better for her. Nope, Roane's method had always been more along the lines of making approving mumbles and hoping he got the message. But in her plane, where she was totally in control of her environment, even giving instructions to a man like Adam Bryant seemed like the most natural thing in the world to her.

Unfortunately the fact it was a man like Adam made her think about what it would be like to give him a different set of instructions. Like a breathless, Kiss me, Adam. Or, Touch me, Adam…

Since when had she been so obsessed with sex?

Feeling the vibration of the engine through the stick Roane stifled a moan, squirming on her seat in an attempt to ease the unfamiliar tension she felt between her legs. Thankfully when she glanced at Adam he seemed engrossed enough with flying not to have noticed so she damped her lips and told him, 'Okay. Now you try.'

His fingers flexed around the stick while Adam took a breath and tried to ignore the move she'd just made—he'd seen that shimmy of her hips on the seat. She was more distracting than the flying lesson.

Of all the things he'd mentally prepared for there had never once been the scenario of being instantly viscerally attracted to his little brother's woman. And woman she was, no matter how much the 'little girl' tag he'd given her as a kid still seemed appropriate. Everything about her was little: little fine-boned hands, little wrists he could circle comfortably with his thumb and forefinger, little waist he could probably have spanned with both hands, little breasts that would easily fill his palms…

Yet everything she did and said belied any air of fragility her body intimated. Not that she came across as tough— quite the opposite. She had an air of vulnerability to her that Adam found compellingly fascinating. Not a bad thing considering where he was.

Adam hated small planes.

Her softly feminine voice filled his ears. 'There you go. You're flying.'

While Adam focused on the combination of what he was doing and his physical awareness of the woman sitting beside him Roane took the silence to mean she could try making conversation again.

'Is it weird being back?'

'At the Vineyard?'

'Yes.'

'No.'

'How can it not be? You've been gone a long time.'

Adam didn't take kindly to being called a liar, even subtextually, frowning as he spoke. '"My witness is the empty sky."'

There was a brief silence.

'Voltaire?'

'Kerouac.'

When he looked sideways at her she was staring at him and Adam liked that she couldn't figure him out. It could stay that way as far as he was concerned.

'You have dozens of these, don't you?'

Adam felt his mouth twitch. 'A few.'

'As a way to avoid making conversation?'

Nope, he could make conversation when he *wanted* to.

'You're not good with silence, then, I take it.'

'I'm fine with silence.' Said the woman who had babbled nervously at him all the way through the airport concourse. 'It's rudeness that bothers me—I'm just trying to figure out if that's what you're doing.'

'So short sentences make me an idiot—the lack of idle conversation makes me rude.' Adam took a breath. 'Anything else?'

There was another moment of silence and then a mumbled, 'You really couldn't be any different from Jake if you tried…'

She might not have meant it with quite the same level of contempt his father had any time he'd used similar words, but they had the same effect. Adam felt the echo of adolescent anger roll in on him like a tsunami—destroying any sense of reason or tolerance in its wake the same way it always had. He'd heard the words a million times; said with impatience or frustration or resentment or in disappointment. But the result was always the same. Jake had been the son their father wanted. Adam had fallen short of the mark.

Well, not any more. Maybe Roane Elliott should be the first of them to understand that.

Adam turned his head, dropping his gaze to look her over at his leisure. He heard her sharp intake of breath when he watched the rise and fall of her breasts long enough to see two distinct beads appear against the soft material of her blouse. Then he smiled a slow smile as he looked up at her parted lips, at the flush on her cheeks and finally into the darkened blue of her eyes. Only then did he quirk his brows, his voice a low rumble in the headsets.

'Ready to find out just how different, little girl?' He angled his head a little and studied the way her honey-blonde hair curled against her cheek. 'I saw how you looked at me on the beach last night. Manners and IQ weren't high on the list of things you were interested in then, were they?'

When she stared at him with widened eyes he leaned a little closer, deliberately looking down the 'V' of her blouse at the rapid rise and fall of creamy half-circle breasts above the lace of her bra. He watched the beating pulse on one side of her elegant neck, the way she damped her parted lips before sucking in a shaky breath. Then his gaze locked firmly with hers again. 'You're right. It *is* about control with me. But you want to lose it, don't you? In a way you obviously don't with my brother or you wouldn't react to me the way you do. You know I'd take you the way you want to be taken. Hard. And slow. For hours on end…'

There was a brief narrowing of her eyes before he continued, 'Maybe you should make sure you chose the right Bryant, little girl…'

Roane's breath caught, she swallowed hard and then her eyes sparkled with a mixture of outrage and desire. 'I'm not some *little girl* you can intimidate.' Her chin lifted defiantly, the husky edge of her voice giving away her physical reaction to his words as much as her body already had. 'Let go of the stick. *Please.*'

Adam frowned. 'Wh—?'

Without warning her knee jerked, and the plane veered violently to the left, throwing Adam away from her. He released the stick as if he'd been burned, his stomach lurching and a violent expletive leaving his mouth. When the plane eased smoothly onto an even keel again he glared angrily at her.

'What did you do?'

Roane was facing forwards, both hands on the stick and her fine-boned jaw-line set with determination. 'I'm sorry. My foot must have slipped.'

Meaning she'd kicked the rudder, right? Adam would have laughed at her audacity if she hadn't just taken a year off his life. His brother had gone and got himself quite the little firecracker.

'Clever.'

The compliment didn't earn him any brownie points. 'Feel free to take your lack of conversational skills to the extreme from here to New York. Or I can give you a demonstration of just what this plane is capable of if you'd prefer…'

Adam knew she wasn't just referring to the plane. She'd clearly told him not to mess with her. It was a nice try, he'd give her that. It would have worked better if she'd denied anything he'd said about wanting to be taken hard and slow and for hours on end…

The knowledge did several things to Adam.

But what it did most was bring out the primal strand to his DNA code. One that now felt a deep seated need to tame her...

Adam had never backed down from a battle of wills. It had been half his problem for most of his life. So she might have got the upper hand on him this time, but she wouldn't do it again. She should understand who she was dealing with. All of them should.

She'd just get a more pleasurable version of the lesson...

CHAPTER THREE

'DO I HAVE TO?'

Jake's brows rose, 'You don't like him much, do you? I thought you liked everyone.'

Under normal circumstances she did. Roane was a glass-half-full kinda gal. Not till Adam had she met anyone who made her believe irredeemable people existed. Feeling that way and being so physically attracted to him at the same time only made her dislike him more than she already did...

But he'd basically called her a gold-digger!

More than that—she was an unfaithful gold-digger who would stoop to having hot, sweaty, emotionless sex with her supposed boyfriend's brother! He was slime. No. He was lower than that. She scowled harder. 'He's not nice.'

Jake stifled a smile, but not convincingly. 'Okay. You got me. What happened on the way down here?'

Ooh...now where to start with that one...?

Idly swinging the office chair back and forth, she searched the air for something safe to say. 'He thought I thought he was an idiot...'

Yes, she was pretty sure it started there. No—hang on—maybe sooner. He hadn't been happy with her knowing he was afraid of flying. 'By the way—did you know he's not good with planes?'

Jake shrugged, flicking through a file on his desk. 'It's not surprising. Hitting the ground harder than normal when you're in one would do it.'

Roane's jaw dropped. 'What?'

'Charter flight, if I remember it right; Adam and his mother were flying in from a week in the Hamptons when Adam was three or four—Dad had visitation rights. It was a rough landing.' He shrugged. 'No one got hurt but it was edge-of-the-seat stuff.'

To a child it must have been a nightmare. No wonder he wasn't a good flier. Would it have killed Adam to possibly mention that? 'Jake, it didn't occur to you he mightn't be that good a flier when you suggested he *fly* down here?'

'He should've said if it was such a big problem.'

'Does he strike you as the kind of man who would confess to a weakness like that in front of a brother he hasn't seen in twelve years? Between the two of you there was enough testosterone in that kitchen this morning to sink a schooner.' There was no way she was getting caught in the middle of that battle of wills so if Jake thought—

He looked up at her. 'Now you're defending him? Thought you didn't like him.'

'I don't.' She fought the need to pout.

'Well, calling him an idiot wasn't one of your better moves. What did he say to that?'

'I didn't call him an idiot. He *assumed* I thought he was. And he was—*surly...*'

Jake chuckled. 'Yeah, I'll bet he was.' He checked his heavy wristwatch and closed the file before pushing his chair back. 'You know he's got a genius level IQ? One fifty or sixty;

something close to the highest level they measure it at. Bugged the hell out of me when I was a kid; made me feel real dumb in comparison.'

'You're kidding me, right?'

'Nope.' He lifted his jacket off the back of his chair and pushed his arms into the dark sleeves. 'Dad reckoned it was part of his restlessness. No matter how many grades he skipped he was still bored. He didn't want to be groomed as a child prodigy, so he rebelled. I think Dad blamed himself for never being able to keep his mind actively interested in anything long enough to stay out of trouble.'

When Jake chuckled at her expression a realization hit her. So Roane dropped her face into her hands, her voice muffled. 'Oh, God.'

'What did you do?'

She peeked over the tips of her fingers, opening them a little so Jake could hear her. 'He quoted Voltaire and Kerouac at me.'

'And you said?'

Dropping her hands, she sighed heavily. 'I asked if they were quote of the day.'

Jake snorted with laughter, then saw her woeful expression and controlled it, his dark eyes still sparkling with amusement as he reached for a hand to draw her out of her chair. 'I can't believe he's here less than twenty-four hours and you've already had a fight with him. You're s'posed to be the friendlier one of the two of us. I have more to argue about with him than you do and *I've* managed to stay calm.'

Yeah, but he didn't have the same issues with Adam she did. Not that she could tell him that.

'Just promise you'll be nice until he signs the papers. Then you can say whatever you want to him. I know I intend to.'

She let Jake guide her to the door. 'Do I have to?'

'You do. For me. If I didn't have you to be nice to guests and clients while I'm up to my eyes in work I'd have to go out and find myself a wife, wouldn't I?'

Roane rolled her eyes. 'Poor you.'

'Exactly.' He held open the door and stepped back to let her through. 'You're as near to an actual Bryant as be damned, Ro, and you know it. That makes it your *duty*.'

When he nodded wisely Roane chuckled, lightly punching his upper arm as he fell into step beside her in the corridor. 'I hate you.'

Jake swatted the back of her head with his file. 'No, you don't. You love me. You know you do. I'm adorable.'

Her smile faded when they rounded a corner and found Adam standing by the doors to the boardroom, his hands pushed deep into the pockets of his dark trousers.

His dark gaze crashed into hers. Immediately she felt a flush rising in her cheeks. Damn him. She really didn't like him one little bit. Regardless of the new information she now had to explain a very small portion of his behaviour.

Feeding the façade, she turned on her heel and stood on tiptoes to press a kiss to Jake's cheek, smiling at the surprise in his eyes. 'I do love you. But you owe me for this one. Big time.'

Jake blinked at her. 'O-kay.'

With a deep breath she turned and walked towards Adam, her chin held high despite the sparkling of silent amusement in his stunning eyes. 'I'll be back after the meeting. Jake tells me you're staying at the penthouse.'

'Will you be acting as tour guide?' He smiled lazily, his deep voice lowering. 'Or making sure I don't skip town again?'

Roane blinked innocently, unable to resist baiting him with a small pout. 'Babysitter possibly?'

Adam's gaze rose to watch the people filtering into the boardroom. Then he took a step closer, invading her personal space to within inches and surrounding her with his enticing scent while he lowered his head.

'Nice to see there's as much fire in your relationship with Jake as there is in ours.' He turned his head closer to her ear so she felt the movement of his lips against her hair. 'Let me know when you're ready to upgrade…'

Roane took a deep breath, ignoring her dancing pulse while she turned her face towards his. 'I'm not so sure it would be an *upgrade*.'

When a smile threatened the corners of his tempting mouth she took another breath, reminding herself that she'd told Jake she would be nice to his brute of a brother. 'Have fun at your board meeting.'

When she impulsively patted his arm, Adam's chin dropped, disbelief lifting his brows and furrowing his forehead when he looked back up at her. It was a very, very small victory, but somehow it was enough for Roane.

His eyes narrowed when she smiled a little brighter, but then Jake interrupted, 'You ready, Adam?'

'Yeah.' He glanced down at Roane. 'Later.'

Roane scrunched up her nose with feigned glee. 'Can't wait.'

Adam had to grit his teeth through the majority of the board meeting. They'd dumbed it down for him. Assuming he wouldn't have a clue about anything they were talking about was a serious mistake on their part. But he remained silent throughout.

Let them think what they wanted.

'So you see the problem.' Jake waited for the room to clear before he turned towards him.

'I do.'

Adam looked at his sibling with new-found respect. The kid knew his stuff. He'd led the meeting with a firm hand and was savvy about every aspect of the company's businesses. Where someone had to open a file to quote figures, Jake was able to correct their mistakes off the top of his head. He gave credit where credit was due for good work, was able to hand out recrimination with a glare. There was no doubt who was the captain of the good ship Bryant. Good for him. Just a shame so many members of his crew were useless.

'And you hire this lot or are they inherited?'

'Some are inherited.'

Adam bet he could name them without Jake's help. 'So cut the dead weight.'

'It's not that simple.'

'Never is.'

'Some of them are shareholders.'

Well that explained that, then. Losing the majority hold on shares was Jake's biggest threat. It was the reason Adam was there. He doubted Jake would have bothered looking for him otherwise. Especially if he knew the truth.

Jake stared calmly at him while Adam moved his head from shoulder to shoulder to ease imaginary tension in his neck. 'What do you want to do, Adam?'

'Are you going to give me options?' Adam stopped what he was doing and looked his brother in the eye. 'See me here with a nice little corner office, do you?'

'No.'

'Good. I've never spent a day of my life in an office, and I'm not starting now.' It would be suffocating.

'You'll sell to me, then.'

'Maybe.' He laid his palms against the gleaming table and

pushed his chair back, stretching his long legs out in front of him. 'Where are you getting the money?'

When Jake studied him with suspicion Adam thought he'd overplayed the nonchalance card. So he leaned forwards, bending his knees so he had a place to rest his forearms. 'It'd take time to liquidate enough assets and you'd need permission from the board for that—which you're not going to get if anyone stands to make any money with a takeover bid. So where would it come from?'

Jake pursed his lips.

So Adam pushed off his knees into an upright position, 'You either want me to have the full picture or you don't.'

'What difference does it make?' Jake's voice remained calm. 'You don't need to know where I get it any more than I need to know what you do with it.'

Fair point. Except he did want to know. If his little brother wasn't going to tell him, then he'd find out on his own.

Adam glanced around the large room, taking in the changes since the days he'd been dragged along for the obligatory heir-to-the-kingdom tours. Instead of heavy oak and opressive panelling there were shining modern surfaces and spotlights immitating stars in a jet-black ceiling. He'd bet his father hadn't initiated the changes, which made him wonder just how long Jake had held the reins. And how much of the conglomerate's current problems were actually his doing…

'Four years.'

Adam looked at Jake.

Who leaned back in his chair and formed a tent with his fingers. 'I've been running it four years. That's what you were wondering.'

Adam hid his surprise at the unexpected spark of insight. 'You were young.'

'I didn't have much of a choice, did I?'

'Everyone has a choice.'

'Not if they give a damn, they don't. Then they make decisions based on what matters. Or what *should* matter.'

Adam shook his head, exhaling a soft snort of derisive laughter as he pushed to his feet. 'Don't pretend to know what mattered or didn't matter to me, Jake. You don't know anything about me.'

'And whose fault is that?' Before Adam could reply Jake pushed to his feet, gathering files together as he continued, 'You might not care about this company, Adam, but I do. So if you're selling, let me know. If you want to learn more before you decide, then say so. The door has always been open.'

He looked Adam in the eye on his way past. 'Whether you thought it was or not.'

Adam stood in the empty room for a while after Jake left. He'd been there one day—hell, not even that long—and already he felt as if the walls were closing in. Dropping his head back, he scowled at the ceiling; it was as if he'd stepped back in time and hadn't learned a single thing in his twelve years away.

Turning on his heel, he dropped his chin—and met Roane's gaze through the vertical blinds. She was standing still in the middle of the bustling hallway, watching him. Lit by the bright light streaming through the office windows, her skin glowed, her hair shone like ripe corn fields in summer sunshine—and wearing a red jacket she stood out in the sea of greys, blacks and charcoals like a beacon.

For a split second he almost smiled at her. But instead he frowned at the fact she might have seen even a hint of how he was feeling. He didn't want anyone to see. It was a weakness. So with a silent mental shake he gathered himself together, stepping out through the doorway and striding confidently towards her, determined to pick up where they'd left off. But before he got to her a middle-aged man from the meeting stepped over.

'Good to see you, Adam.' His voice was laced with thinly veiled disrespect. 'We thought you were dead.'

Adam was a step away from him when he stopped. He clenched his jaw. Talking a measured step backwards, he turned his face towards the man, his voice cold. 'Sorry to disappoint.' He looked him over. 'Jeffries, right?'

The man swallowed hard. 'That's right.'

Adam nodded, slowly turning ninety degrees to tower over him. 'Well...*Jeffries*...a word to the wise...'

He paled. 'Y-yes?'

'Ever treat me like a fool the way you did in that meeting again and you'll wish I *was* dead.' When he lifted his arm the man flinched, and Adam smiled inwardly as he swiped an imaginary piece of lint off his shoulder before lowering his head to add, 'Have a nice day.'

Roane blinked wide eyes at him as he walked by her, her voice choked. 'Bye, Malcolm.'

'Roane...' Malcolm Jeffries was too busy scurrying away to pay much attention to her.

A quick glance over Adam's shoulder told him she was following him to the elevators, so he punched the button and waited. When she got to his side Adam glanced sideways at her, 'You got something to say, then spit it out.'

'Nope. Nothing to say.'

'Good.'

'Except he probably deserved it,' she said after a moment of silence. 'Malcolm can be a bit of a jerk. Office lech too, from what the girls say. Wandering hands...'

Adam's face jerked her way so fast he almost put his neck out. 'He *touched* you?'

One arched brow rose as she rolled back onto her heels. 'That would be your problem because?'

Damned if Adam knew. But it took a gargantuan effort not to turn round and go right back down the hall for another tête-à-tête. The elevator better get a move on. He glanced up at the numbers: forty-two, forty-three... It was the slowest elevator in New York.

'Jake didn't have a quiet word?' Bitterness rolled off the tip of his tongue. But if he hadn't, then he'd just dropped in Adam's estimation.

'Why would he—? Oh...' When she faltered Adam turned to study her expression, the fact she wasn't able to look him in the eye making him suspicious even before a hint of colour started to appear on her cheeks. 'I didn't say he touched me—I said the office girls mentioned it. It wouldn't have been Jake's problem even if he had. I can look after myself.'

Adam turned towards her, calmly folding his arms, 'Anything else you want to set straight?'

She looked up at him, her luminous blue eyes filled with curiosity. 'How come you didn't tell me the reason you don't like flying?'

She'd been asking questions about him, had she? That was interesting, but, 'That wasn't what I meant.'

She blinked blankly at him.

One of the things Roane Elliott needed to learn about him quick smart was that he wasn't that easily diverted. 'Are you or are you not involved with Jake?'

'I am.' She nodded firmly.

Adam knew he'd worded it wrong. *'Sexually.'*

Her eyes widened, gaze darting nervously around them and her voice lowering. 'Do you *mind*?'

As it happened, yes, he did. He minded a whole heap.

They stepped into the elevator together, Adam waiting until the doors closed before he moved and effectively boxed her into a corner with his body.

'Yes or no.'

The small space between them seemed to crackle. From the change in her breathing and the sharp intake of breath she took Adam knew she could feel it as keenly as he could. He couldn't remember the last time he'd felt so much heat radiating from a woman. He'd felt it on the beach, he'd felt it in the kitchen, he'd provoked it on the plane…

If she wasn't involved with Jake, then she was in way over her pretty little head. She was exactly the kind of distraction Adam needed from the things he currently felt he had a fleeting control over.

The doors behind him slid open and he saw Roane angling her head to look around him, the small grimace on her face telling him they had company. So he casually leaned a shoulder against the wall and lowered his tone.

'Yes or no.'

Roane glared at him, answering in a similarly low tone, 'None of your business.'

'I'm making it my business.'

'Why?' She seemed astounded by the notion.

Surely she couldn't be that naive? But if she wanted to have the discussion in front of an audience, then so be it. 'Why do you think?'

Taking a moment to smile weakly at the other occupant of the elevator, she flicked her long lashes upwards again. 'I'm not interested.'

Adam's smile was slow. 'Liar.'

The elevator doors opened again and for a brief second Adam thought he heard her moan. Probably mentally willing their visitor to stay. But by the time the doors closed the spark of fire had returned to her eyes.

'I *meant* I didn't want to know why.' She cocked her head to one side, the curls at the end of her shoulder-length hair brushing the collar of her jacket. Then she grumbled, 'If your ego gets any bigger you'll have to give it its own name.'

'So why did you tell me you're in a relationship with my brother if you're not?'

Roane growled at him. '*You* are the most—'

Adam calmly folded his arms again. 'Want to know what I think?'

She lifted her arms and flopped them down into a similar folded position, pouting in a way that drew his attention to her mouth. 'No.'

Adam continued to stare at her mouth. 'I think you were hiding behind him.'

When she worried on her lower lip it drew his hand out of the crook of his arm, his thumb pressing against it to still the movement. 'Don't do that.'

When his gaze rose he found her staring at him, the blue now clouded with—he frowned—was it fear? It made him study her closer, the realization slow to filter through to the front of his brain. 'This is new to you.'

How could someone with so much fire not have experience of sexual attraction on its most basic level? There was no way she'd got to her age and not— He almost laughed in disbelief at the idea. There was no way she was a virgin.

When the doors slid open he dropped his hand and glanced over his shoulder, frowning when they were joined by several men and women in suits. He knew there was another reason he hated office environments. Too many damn people.

He looked down at Roane again, the flush on her cheeks and the laboured rise and fall of her breasts telling him just how affected she was by their topic of conversation and the proximity he'd forced on her. There was one thing he was sure of— she *was* turned on. He'd bet she was ready for him already.

He breathed deep as if he might catch the scent of her arousal in the air, then stated the obvious with deep satisfaction. 'It's a no to you and Jake.'

'Well, that genius IQ obviously isn't wasted on you, is it?' She glared up at him, then looked away.

'Was it ever a yes?'

'No. Happy now?' Another glare.

Ecstatic. For the first time since he'd laid eyes on her Adam let go. He experienced anticipation thrumming through his veins, the rush of adrenalin pumping his blood harder. It had been a long, long time since he'd been so turned on by the thrill of the chase.

He wanted her. He wanted her bad. Adam always got what he wanted. Had done for a long, long time. He'd built his new life on his ability to make things happen…and on never taking no for an answer…

Roane's gaze flickered upwards, her eyes widened and then she whispered huskily, 'Please stop that.'

'Stop what?' he whispered back, leaning in a little closer and allowing his gaze to drop to her mouth.

The mouth she dutifully prepared for him with the tip of her tongue. 'You know what.'

Yes, he did. He knew exactly what he was doing.

The doors slid open at street level, so Adam pushed his

shoulder off the wall and waited for the other occupants to leave before swinging an arm in invitation. 'Miss Elliott.'

She glared sideways at him on her way past.

He fell into step beside her, matching his long-legged stride to her fast paced clicking of heels on the sheen of the foyer floor. Then he let her go through the swinging doors first, his gaze dropping to the rounded curve of her rear.

On the bustling sidewalk of Park Avenue he casually reached for her elbow, swinging her sharply around. Her hair arced out from her head, she scowled in annoyance. Then Adam hauled her in, pressing his mouth to hers.

When she tried to pull back he lifted his other hand, wrapping his fingers around the back of her head and adding enough pressure to still her. She moaned in complaint. He smiled against her lips. She was the sweetest thing he'd ever tasted. All the sweeter because she didn't fight.

Her lips were warm and soft beneath his, full and irresistibly inviting. When she didn't open to let him in he sucked her lower lip between his, teasing it with the tip of his tongue. Her sharp gasp garnered such a deep sense of victory in him he did it again, purposefully keeping the kiss soft and persuasive—lips coaxing as his tongue caressed. She shivered, he nipped her lower lip. Silently demanding she succumb to him.

Roane made a strangled noise in the base of her throat. When she opened her lips to let the noise out, Adam dipped the tip of his tongue into her mouth, curling it to tease the tip of hers. Suddenly she was leaning into him as if her legs couldn't quite hold her up… It was all he needed to make his point. For now.

He dragged his mouth from hers and set her back a step, smiling as she swayed and her heavy-lidded eyes gradually blinked him into focus.

'I can find the penthouse on my own unless they've moved it since my day.'

Her brows wavered, her breathing laboured as questions formed in her expressive eyes. 'Why did— How— You can't—'

Adam pressed his forefinger to her mouth, lowering his head to look deep into her eyes. 'Just something for you to think about, little girl.'

Roane began to frown, but Adam smiled lazily. The battle lines were drawn now.

He moved the tip of a blunt fingernail over her swollen lower lip, his gaze watching the movement as he told her in a low, rumbling voice, 'When you've thought about it you'll find me. Or I'll find you. It's that simple.'

Roane blinked at him with wide eyes.

Good girl. That's more like it. He rewarded her with a small smile, his voice low and steeped with promises of what was to come. 'It's gonna be hot, little girl—trust me. This kinda chemistry? It's rare.'

Then he dropped his hand and turned on his heel, letting a full-blown smile loose as he walked away…

CHAPTER FOUR

HE WAS SITTING in a café when Roane caught sight of him hours later, his elbows on the table and his chin resting in the palm of one large hand while he looked ahead.

He looked as if he had a lot on his mind. If he'd been anyone else she knew Roane would immediately have walked over and pulled out a chair to talk to him. But he was Adam. She didn't want to help him feel better when he'd walked away before she could form a sentence!

Why-oh-why did it have to be *Adam* who kissed her better than she'd ever been kissed before? Who left her standing on the same spot long after he'd walked away—blinking while she tried to figure out why it suddenly felt as if the world had tilted on its axis beneath her feet. And that it was a man like Adam who had done it was just…it was…well…it just didn't make any sense to Roane. She didn't even *like him*.

He was arrogant, blunt to the point of rudeness, overbearing… She had a long list of what he was.

Pursing her lips and scrunching up her nose, Roane turned on her heel to walk away. She didn't care what was on his mind.

A whimper of frustration sounded low in her throat as she wavered on the balls of her feet—trying to force herself to walk away. If she went over there he would just be Adam. It had taken her the rest of the afternoon and most of the evening wandering around Manhattan to feel like herself again.

She grimaced, attempted to go left and bumped shoulders with someone. 'I'm so sorry.'

She tried going right and managed two steps before she stopped again, stamping her foot in frustration. She really had had enough. Adam Bryant needed to understand he couldn't just stride in on those long legs of his and ride roughshod over her. She wasn't going to be bullied, or intimidated or harassed or—*tempted,* darn it. He needed to get that.

She needed to have the guts to tell him.

Yanking determinedly on the bottom of her fitted jacket, she turned on her heel and marched across the street to his table.

'We need to get a few things straight.'

His hand dropped from his chin, ridiculously thick lashes shifting upwards as he looked at her with a confident calmness that made her want to slap him. 'Pull up a chair…'

When he jerked his chin at the chair in front of her Roane frowned down at it, then looked back up, a thought sidetracking her. 'You got changed.'

When she'd left him he'd been wearing the dark suit he'd looked so good in, now he was in jeans and a dark navy T-shirt that he looked just as good in. But she didn't remember him having a bag with him.

How could one man look that good in every item of clothing he ever wore?

'I picked something up.' He reached over and pulled the chair out. 'Sit.'

Roane had to move back a step to make room for it. 'See, that's one of the things we need to talk about—you can't keep giving me orders. I don't work for you.'

'You're on the Bryant payroll, aren't you?'

'Yes, but—'

'Well, contrary to popular belief I'm still a Bryant, so therefore by default…' he pulled the chair further out '…you *do* work for me. Sit.'

She didn't want to sit. 'If I worked for you I'd probably be looking into a harassment suit about now. I really don't appreciate being talked to the way you talk to me. It's—'

'Rude; yes, you said. Don't sit then. What do you want to drink?'

'I don't want a drink.' She frowned at him when he looked around for a waitress.

'Nothing quite like sitting outside with a cold one in New York City on a warm night, is there? Sit here long enough and you'll see the world go by.'

Roane had always thought that too, but even so… 'I don't know where it is you've been the last twelve years, but back here in civilization—'

'I moved around a lot. In the last few years I've split my time between the places I liked best: San Francisco, New Orleans, here…'

Here? He'd been in New York? But that didn't make sense. 'Why didn't you visit your family if you were close by?'

Adam shrugged. 'Never got round to it.'

A cop-out if ever she heard one. 'Didn't it occur to you they might want to know you were still alive?'

'If anything happened to me they'd have been told. I have strict instructions laid down. I had a lot of things written down after Katrina…'

Roane's eyes widened when she put two and two together from what he'd said. '*Hurricane* Katrina?'

'Yep.' He grinned, dazzling her with perfectly straight

white teeth before he winked. 'Now there was a gal to make you think long and hard about life.'

Roane blinked at him while he smiled at the waitress, who smiled in return. 'Same again.'

'You got it.'

Adam raised his brows at Roane, who gave him a wide-eyed glare of recrimination before glancing down at the beer bottle in front of him. She sighed heavily before drawing the chair back the last few inches. 'I'll have what he's having.'

When she was seated Adam leaned back, his forearms resting on the table while he idly turned the bottle in circles between his long fingers. 'Never tempted to leave the island?'

'I like it there.'

'There's a big wide world out here, little girl—didn't you want to see any of it?'

'I still have a few years left. And I've never been all that keen on the idea of hurricanes myself...'

Adam's mouth quirked, his gaze rising from the bottle to study her face. 'Planning on leaving it till retirement, are you? I hope we got you a good pension plan in that employment contract.'

'You did. The family more than looks after me; they have done for a long time.' She folded her arms and flumped petulantly back into her chair. Why was she sitting having a drink with him? How had that happened?

'Does your dad still work the estate?'

Roane felt the familiar sense of loss at the mention of the man she still missed so badly. 'He died three years ago. He had a heart attack.'

'I'm sorry.'

The softer tone to his deep voice brought another ache to Roane's chest, but she shrugged. 'It happens.'

'He was a good man. We used to talk some.'

Her gaze was accusatory. 'I don't remember that.'

'You wouldn't. You were either at school or tagging around after Jake like a puppy.'

'I did *not* tag around after Jake like a puppy.' They'd been joined at the hip for a long time, yes, but he made it sound as if she'd had some kind of schoolgirl crush on him. 'We were *friends*. We still are.'

'That's not how I remember it.'

'I remember you as a latter-day James Dean who didn't give a damn about anything or anyone—how accurate an assessment was *that*?' She jerked her brows.

Lifting his bottle, he tilted it in salute.

When he set the lip to his mouth Roane took the opportunity to notice a few things. Like the two thin strips of leather knotted around his wrist, a matching one tied round his neck and disappearing into the neck of his T-shirt, the wide silver band on the ring finger of his right hand...how his throat convulsed as he swallowed...the flicker of his tongue over his wide mouth to remove any lingering moisture...

Then her gaze rose and met his again, the green in his eyes merging into the brown with silent knowing. He'd seen her checking him out, hadn't he? Well, he could think what he wanted—she hadn't been thinking about the kiss. *Much.*

The waitress reappeared with their drinks, setting napkins down before she removed the bottles from her circular tray and bestowed a wide smile on Adam for his word of thanks.

Roane lifted hers, wiped the top with the napkin and took a sip, frowning at how easily he seemed to have charmed the brunette. He liked to keep his options open, didn't he? That really shouldn't have bugged her as much as it did, but—

She looked around, the sound of distant sirens and a loudly honking horn telling her a fire truck was going to work a few blocks away—then she glanced at Adam and found him studying her with hooded eyes.

'What?'

'You're mad at yourself for sitting down, aren't you?'

She sighed in exasperation. 'Who wouldn't want to spend time in your charming company?'

A lazy smile curled his mouth, deepening the grooves in his cheeks. 'You really don't like me much, do you?'

'You've not given me much of a reason to.'

'You just don't know me well enough yet.'

'And you're planning on sticking around long enough for that to happen, are you?'

Shifting his gaze to the people on the sidewalk behind her, he shrugged again. 'I haven't decided what I'm doing yet.'

Something in his tone made Roane delve into an area that really wasn't any of her business. 'How did it go with your father this morning?'

'He didn't know me.'

Roane grimaced inwardly because it had to have hurt, even after so many years. How could it not? Her voice softened as a result. 'Mornings aren't good for him. Until he gets into the routine of the day he can be disorientated—and in fairness it'll have been a surprise to him. He doesn't do well with surprises. If we'd known you were coming home we could have prepared him for a few days to—'

Adam looked sideways at her. 'Spend a lot of time with the old man, do you?'

'Yes.' She wasn't put off by the flat tone of his voice. 'We all share the time between us. We have to. It's a full-time job.'

He looked back at the crowd.

But Roane still felt the need to help. 'He'll know you. Give it time. He talks about you every day.'

The burst of low laughter was bitter. 'Yeah, I'll bet he does.'

She shook her head, confused. 'Why come back if you hate him so much?'

He frowned as if he wasn't happy saying the words out loud. 'I'm here for me, not him.'

Edward Bryant wasn't an easy man, Roane knew that. But neither had she any experience of him being as awful as Adam seemed to think he was. She'd always thought he was more of a pussy cat inside than he let the world see. Roane being Roane, she immediately felt the need to try and mediate in some way. A father and his son should never be as estranged as they were.

She couldn't stop the words from slipping free. 'It must have been quite the bust up you had with him…'

Adam smiled wryly as he lifted his bottle to his mouth. 'It wasn't exactly an episode of *The Waltons,* let's put it that way.'

'You used to argue a lot. I remember that.' There had been times when their raised voices could be heard echoing through the large house, times when Jake had frowned and dragged her outside into the open air where they couldn't hear it. Adam might not have known it, but those arguments had upset his kid brother just as much as they probably had him— maybe more—because Adam's leaving had placed a rift between the father and his second son too…

Again it probably wasn't her place, but he needed to hear it. 'Jake blamed him for you leaving.'

Adam's head turned sharply. 'I was always going to leave. It was just a question of when.'

'Why?'

His brows lifted in disbelief. 'Why?'

'Yes. Why?'

Adam was staring at her as if she'd just dropped in from another planet. 'You think it's that simple? I'm supposed to spill my guts and you'll dish out some words of wisdom to make everything all right? I'm going to lay my head on your shoulder afterwards and we can shed a few tears—share a chick-flick moment. Is that how you see this working out?'

She smiled at him. 'Yet after one itty bitty kiss I'm s'posed to fall at your feet and jump straight into bed with you. That any simpler, is it?'

To her amazement he smiled back, nodding his head and pursing his lips as he lifted his bottle again. 'I get it. You're here to psychoanalyze me in search of redeeming qualities. Then you'll feel better about being attracted to me.'

'I think you want me to hate you.' She lifted her own bottle. 'It's the easy way out. Sex for sex's sake and you don't ever have to get involved with anyone, right?'

'Well, you know what they say, sweetheart: it's better to be hated for what you are than loved for something you're not…' He had the gall to continue smiling at her over the lip of the bottle. 'You're still not denying you're attracted to me though, are you? Hate me all you want. It's just going to make it all the hotter when it happens.'

Roane set her bottle back down with a dull thud.

Before she could say anything Adam leaned closer, his voice low. 'Ever have angry sex, little girl? I'm betting you haven't. I'm betting there's plenty you haven't tried. That's what's got you here when you don't want to be, isn't it?'

His gaze shifted, his head angling so he could study her closer. 'There's a part of you—deep down inside—that wants to experience what you've never experienced before. I'm the key to a door you've never dared open. But you're burning with curiosity to know what's on the other side, aren't you?'

Roane's mouth was as dry as a desert, her throat raw when she attempted to swallow. She could feel the heat building inside her body, could feel her skin tingling as if it were being touched by the whisper of his seductive words. Heaven help her. Everything he said was true. She burned. And he hadn't laid a finger on her.

His gaze slid leisurely down the V of her jacket to the breasts that immediately seemed to swell against the confines of lace cups. 'You want to know what it's like to have my hands on you—to have my mouth on your skin—what it'll feel like when I'm inside y—'

'*Stop.*' She exhaled the word on a note of pure agony, her heart slamming against her breastbone. No one had ever spoken to her the way he was. The fact it was seriously doing things for her was shocking. She'd never thought of herself as the kind of girl who was turned on by a man who could talk dirty.

Adam's gaze rose sharply to search her wide eyes. 'Why so scared? That's what I don't get. You're too old to be a virgin. You're curious or you wouldn't be here. You can't tell me you're not turned on. Like I said before, I'm not an idiot.'

Roane forced her vocal cords to work. 'You *are* the most arrogant man I've ever met.'

'Not arrogance, sweetheart—*confidence.* Life experience brings you that, along with a healthy dose of "life's too short." You want this as much as I do. You know you do. Why fight it?'

'Why?' The whispered question rose up from deeper inside her than she'd ever looked before. '*Why me?*'

Surprise flickered across his hypnotic eyes. '*Why?*'

Roane could only manage a nod.

To her utter astonishment, one large hand lifted to push her hair back and cradle the side of her head, his thumb smoothing over the skin on her cheek with impossible gentleness. Then his deep voice rumbled low. 'I'll tell you why, little girl; it's because I want to be the one to teach you the things you've obviously been missing out on.'

Roane blinked at him in wonder.

The smile he gave her was devilishly slow and sexy, creating a coiling knot low in her abdomen. 'Life should be filled with unforgettable experiences. I promise I'd make this one of them for you.'

Roane was drowning in a sea of seduction so deep she could barely breathe, her very soul yearning for an *unforgettable* sexual experience. She wanted to be shown what all the fuss was about, why some people spent days in bed, what it was that had driven the human race to such extremes in the name of passion. The kind of passion she'd never come close to experiencing; not that she hadn't tried, but she'd been left feeling empty and, well—*unfulfilled,* quite frankly.

Just *once* in her lifetime. Was that so very much to ask? She didn't think it was.

Adam was the perfect candidate if she decided to do something as completely crazy as accept the offer. Not only was he hotter than Hades, he wasn't the kind of man to put her through all the angst and self-doubt of dating. He wouldn't ask for any kind of a commitment. Not liking his personality meant there wasn't any chance of her falling for him and having her heart broken…

All right, so call her shallow; part of her attraction to him was the way he looked—she wouldn't even try to pretend it wasn't. Having such an astonishingly good-looking man pursue her was an undeniable thrill. She was only human.

After an endless moment, she found herself silently nodding, a curl of apprehension tying into a knot in her stomach when his eyelids grew heavy and his smile turned dangerous.

He's going to kiss me again, she realized instinctually. A second later his gaze dropped to her mouth and she knew she was right, her pulse dancing in anticipation and her tongue flickering out to dampen her lips in preparation.

Hurry up and do it, then! She needed to know the first one hadn't been a fluke, made memorable by the element of surprise. It wasn't too late to back out. Women changed their minds all the time.

Adam moved his hand, nudging her chin up with his fist. Then he kissed her. He took advantage of her submission to part her lips with his tongue and sweep inside, taking her sharp gasp of cooler night air and replacing it with raw heat. In a mist of sensuality Roane was only vaguely aware of him wrapping his arm around her waist and tugging her closer to the edge of her chair. Her arms lifted, hands sliding around the column of his neck to hold him tight as their knees bumped together. Every doubt, every fear, every voice of reason in her head short-circuited except one.

Why haven't I been kissed like this before?

It was *so* unfair. Twenty-four hours ago she'd thought she was happy, contented even. That her life was exactly what she wanted it to be. Now she knew what she'd been missing. She felt cheated. If this was just the kissing part, then *heaven help her...*

So much for changing her mind. It was already too late. Her body knew what it craved.

Tentatively she kissed him back, her moves becoming bolder when a growling noise of approval vibrated deep in his chest. She parted her knees and tugged herself closer, feeling the erotic sensation of the rough seams of his jeans sliding up the insides of her soft cotton trousers. But it wasn't enough. Somewhere in her darkest thoughts came the idea— no, the *need*—to climb onto his lap and press her breasts tight against the wall of his chest.

One kiss and she was ready for the kind of public display she would never even have contemplated before.

With considerable effort she leaned back, running her tongue over her swollen lips the second they parted from his. As if subliminally she felt the need to lap up every last taste of him before she opened her eyes.

When she did Adam was staring at her. 'Quick study, aren't you?'

Roane smiled a little shyly. 'You think?'

'I *know*.' He released her and lifted his hands to hers, freeing her fingers from behind his neck. Then he placed his hands on either side of her waist and lifted her up and back— dropping her unceremoniously into place before he pointed a long index finger.

'Stay there. Before you get us both arrested for public indecency.'

When he reached for his beer bottle and downed half its contents Roane's smile grew. 'You started it.'

Adam looked at her from the corner of narrowed eyes, 'Careful, little girl. Or this is gonna happen faster than you're ready for.'

Squirming a little on her seat, she felt her cheeks warming at just *how* ready she was...

Adam's voice was gravelly. *'Quit that.'*

Roane's cheeks burned, so she aimed a scowl at him, 'I'm confused. One minute you're all "I'm gonna teach you" and now you're telling me to behave?'

The beer bottle froze halfway to his mouth, was lowered carefully to the table—then Adam turned at the waist and looked her in the eye. 'As of now lesson number one is about anticipation. I'm going to make sure you're so ready for this you'll go insane if it doesn't happen.'

Roane couldn't help it; she gulped.

Adam slowly nodded his head, 'Mmm-hmm. Lesson two has a lot to do with lesson one; sex isn't just about the body—it's about the mind. It's the largest erogenous zone the body has.'

Said the guy with the genius-level IQ? Roane's brows wavered. Oh she was in *so* much trouble. How was she supposed to compete with that? How did a girl like her engage the mind of someone like him?

The smile started in his eyes. 'What?'

Roane had never been all that good at hiding things. Jake had teased her countless times about wearing her heart on her sleeve and saying a million words with just one look. But Adam didn't know her that well.

'Nothing.'

'Liar.'

She felt a hint of a headache forming behind her eyes. He was hard work. 'You're obviously more experienced with this than I am…'

When she waved a limp-wristed hand in the space between them Adam smiled indulgently. '*Obviously.* Though frankly? Your lack of experience baffles me.'

Roane frowned a little. 'It does?'

'Yes.' For a moment he looked as if he was holding back

a larger smile, then he controlled it and studied her face with open curiosity. 'The island's population jumps from what? Fifteen thousand off season to a hundred thousand in the summer—give or take? You can't tell me there haven't been opportunities.'

Well, yes, there had, but, 'It makes for short-term relationships, though, don't you think?'

'Meaning there *were* opportunities…'

'Not everyone looks at people from the point of view of whether or not there'd be great sex,' said the girl who probably wouldn't know great sex if it drove over her in a bus with the words 'great sex' written on the sidings.

Adam blinked a couple of times. 'So you've been waiting around for Mr. Right. You should know from the get-go— I'm not him.'

'*Obviously.*' The corners of her mouth twitched.

'I mean it. Don't fall for me.'

Roane rolled her eyes. 'Do you ever actually listen to what comes out of your mouth? I mean, *seriously*?'

'Just laying out the ground rules…'

'Uh-huh.' She blinked at him. 'Do I get a say in any of these ground rules?'

'That depends.'

'On what?'

'On whether or not I like what I hear…' he smiled in challenge as he lifted his bottle to his lips again, eyes sparkling at her '…though never let it be said I'm not open to suggestions…'

When he waggled his brows a burst of incredulous laughter left Roane's mouth. 'You're unbelievable.'

'I told you you'd learn to like me when you knew me better.'

That was just it, though. She couldn't. Not if she stood any chance of coming out of the other end of whatever they were doing with her heart still intact. It was a survival thing.

Adam Bryant was *way* out of her league…

CHAPTER FIVE

ADAM TOOK AS deep a breath as his lungs would allow, his chin low and his gaze focused straight ahead. He could beat this. He'd been in New Orleans when the full force of a furious Mother Nature had sent the world crashing down around his ears so he could most certainly beat the violent need to throw up when faced with a pretty little blue and white light aircraft.

Ignoring the trickle of cold sweat working its way down his spine, he set his shoulders. *Mind over matter.*

'I checked the weather; we might hit a little light turbulence before the approach to the Vineyard, but that's it...' Roane's voice was softly feminine and confident at the same time.

But still smacked of sympathy to Adam.

'We could have another flying lesson, if you like.'

He looked at her from the corner of his eye. 'Yes because the last one ended so well for me.'

Roane looked back up at him with sparkling blue eyes, her teeth catching one side of her lower lip before a smile broke free. 'Well, you see, last time you didn't understand the most important ground rule. Or sky rule.' She shifted her gaze upwards and considered that for a moment. 'I'm not quite sure which one it is when we're up there…'

They stopped at the tip of one wing, Adam turning to look down at her. 'Okay, I'll bite. What's the rule?'

Her chin jerked up and a more mischievous smile appeared. 'Up there, *I'm* in control—you're on my turf—any control I give you is on my terms. Therefore rubbing me up the wrong way isn't the brightest move you could make.'

When she added a determined nod to the end of the sentence Adam lifted a brow. She was sassy when she set her mind to it. Adam had always been a sucker for sassy. And feisty. And frisky. Frisky most of all…nothing quite like a frisky woman, he felt…

He allowed himself another leisurely examination of what she was wearing—his sixth or seventh since she'd met him that morning. Again he wondered how she'd managed to stay so inexperienced. The woman dressed in a way that suggested she was way more sexually confident than she actually was.

Not that she was blatantly sexual in the way she dressed. Knowing what he did of her, he knew the very fact it was sexual was probably unintentional. Being five feet five at best, she chose heels to boost her height, heels that made her walk the way women did in heels: with the gentle sway of hips that drew a man's attention. Then there was the way they made her legs appear longer, the zips and tassels on her low-hipped burgundy combat trousers inviting a man's imagination to explore, unzip, untie…*remove*…

But it was her jacket that had him most fascinated. She had a thing about fitted jackets. Bit buttoned down for Adam's preference under normal circumstances, but on Roane they were different—they cinched in at her impossibly small waist, lovingly hugged her pert breasts… created the kind of silhouette that said she might be small, but *man* was she beautifully formed.

The one she was wearing was a dark purple, long-sleeved, high-collared, with seams that ran vertically to highlight that tempting silhouette. Fairly conservative, until she was facing forwards—then it changed completely. Large circular rings lined the front edges, but Roane had left the hooks that held those edges together undone at the top and the bottom. There wasn't just the tempting V down to the valley of her breasts, but an even more tempting inverted V at the bottom that showed mesmerizing glimpses of the feminine curve of her stomach. It made Adam's palms itch to reach out and touch, to push the edges back so he could splay his fingers and feel how soft her skin was.

But if he touched he knew he wouldn't stop. Not when merely looking at her was enough to have his body thrumming with awareness and his jeans too tight for comfort.

Roane hooked her thumbs into the belt loops of her trousers, cocking her hip just enough for him to drag his gaze back up to her face. She lifted an accusatory brow at him.

'Is there any chance you could stop looking at me like I'm chocolate-coated?'

'Actually, that I could work with…' His gaze tangled with hers. 'I did say I was open to suggestions.'

When her mouth dropped open he blinked lazily, allowing his gaze to rove down over her body and back up, 'You should be used to it when you dress like that…'

Her chin dropped. 'What's wrong with it?'

'Oh, sweetheart, there's nothin' *wrong* with it.' He felt his body grow painfully hard as another thought occurred to him. 'You're wearing something under that jacket, right?'

There was a moment of hesitation and then she looked up at him from beneath long lashes. 'It doesn't really need anything under it.'

He was half a step closer when she grabbed hold of his wrist and turned him towards the plane, her voice firmer. 'If it helps to distract you from flying, then you can wonder if I have on any underwear at all. Knowing you, that should keep your mind occupied…'

'Remember we talked about you pushing me?'

'Oh, I remember.' She opened the door to the cockpit and stepped back to make room for him. 'But you also said the mind was the largest erogenous zone. Maybe I'm just testing that theory.'

'You know what they say about payback, don't you?'

'I'd heard a rumour. Get in the plane, please.'

When she let go of his wrist he folded his arms and studied her face with hooded eyes. 'And once I'm in there you're in control.'

'Uh-huh.'

He stepped closer. 'I have to do whatever you say.'

'You do.'

Adam thought it over for a second, his fear of flying taking a back seat to a sudden plethora of possibilities. 'Okay, then.'

Unfolding his arms, he set his hands on her hips; his thumbs on the curve of her stomach as he yanked her closer. When he dipped his thumbs beneath the waistband of her trousers her eyes darkened, the muscles in her abdomen trembling. 'If you're looking to distract me I have a challenge for you…'

Her eyes widened with a sexual awareness she didn't try to hide from him. Learning already, wasn't she?

Adam smiled a slow smile. 'What I want to know is just how far you're prepared to stretch this window of opportunity.

'Cause call me weak, sweetheart—but I'm not prepared to chance another *accidental slip* of your foot on the rudder…'

Roane looked repentant. 'You deserved it.'

'Maybe.'

'No maybe about it—you were an ass.'

'You rattled my cage—' his fingers tightened on her hips '—so if I'm stepping onto your turf and relinquishing control I'd like to know just how far you're prepared to go to distract me this time…'

Curiosity shimmered across her expressive eyes. 'What exactly are you suggesting?'

'It's a one-time offer. I'm putting myself in your hands. Consider it lesson number three…'

She watched as his arms returned to his sides, unable to believe what he was saying judging by her expression. 'Wouldn't you prefer it if I devoted my attention to flying the plane?'

'You said clear skies for most of the way.'

'I did.' Her voice was filled with caution.

'Well, then, you can use that autopilot thing of yours again, can't you?' He rocked forwards and quirked his brows in challenge. 'And a little imagination…'

Her eyes widened. 'You're asking me to—'

'Take charge. Yes, I am.' He rocked back and nodded firmly. 'I'm guessing that's something you've never done with a man before.'

The familiar flush on her cheeks was answer enough.

'Yeah, I thought so. You've never told a man what you wanted or what felt good. Consider this a test run. In the air I'm your temporary slave—emphasis on the word temporary. *Remember that.*'

The uncertainty radiating from her was palpable, so Adam

reached out and tilted her chin up, his voice as low as he could allow it to go to still be heard over the ambient airport sounds surrounding them. 'Do anything you want. Or don't…and I'll just go right ahead and focus on how much I hate planes…'

One small hand shoved him hard in the centre of his chest. '*That's* emotional blackmail.'

'If you say so.'

'I should white-knuckle you from here to the Vineyard for that—it would serve you right.'

'But you won't.' He stepped back and rubbed his palms together vigorously. 'Can't say I've ever looked forward to a flight as much as I am right this second…'

Roane stood on the tarmac for a while after he folded his large frame into the cockpit. She frowned as she closed the door behind him. Then she took her time walking around the tail, glad she'd completed her pre-flight check before he got there. There was no way she'd be able to concentrate properly after his challenge. And challenge it was.

More than he could know.

He was leaving it all down to her: the method of distraction, the execution of it—he wasn't going to do *anything?* So if she wanted to touch him he would just sit there and let her? If she wanted to kiss him he wouldn't kiss her back? Or he would but he wouldn't initiate it?

It was like being given a tiger to play with.

But, boy, was it tempting!

It would just be so much easier to give into temptation if there weren't a very real chance of her making a complete fool of herself. What did she know about seducing a man?

Imagination, he'd said. Okay. She just needed to think about it for a bit. She would focus on the everyday business of getting them safely into the air and out of New York airspace and by the time they got to clearer skies she might have had a stroke of genius.

Mentally she crossed her fingers as she stepped into the cockpit. 'Buckle up, Bryant.'

'Yes, ma'am.'

Roane shook her head as he saluted her.

It was the low tuneless whistling that eventually galvanized her to action. Apparently even thinking about what she might come up with had been enough to settle Adam's nerves. He'd only gripped his knees a little during take-off, swiped his palms a couple of times as they'd ascended to their designated altitude, been pursing his lips just enough for her to know he wasn't one hundred per cent comfortable. Roane found each and every one of the telltale signs endearing. *Worryingly...*

But the whistling made her crazy. 'That sound is magnified in the headsets, you know.'

'What sound?'

'You're whistling.'

'Am I?' He stretched as much as the cockpit would allow. 'Must be passing the time till my distraction gets here...'

'You can be as irritating as a rag-nail when you put your mind to it,' Roane complained beneath her breath, checking all the readouts before she reached for the autopilot. Then she turned to consider him, her mind reaching for a possible solution in the absence of any imagination. What to do... hmm...and how to do it without giving away just how nervous she was?

Adam turned her way, resting his back against the door while he smiled a smile that softened the green in his sensational eyes. 'Don't know what to do, do you?'

'I'm weighing up the options.'

'Chicken.'

She cocked a brow and angled her head. 'I can make you reach for a sick bag in about thirty seconds, you know. The Meridian is a versatile little plane.'

When his eyes sparkled with light she found it hard to stop the smile from making its way onto her face. Darn it. Even when she was supposedly in charge he still had the upper hand on her. Then somewhere out of left field came a glimmer of an idea. Work with what you've got, they said. She'd always found flying sexy so maybe she just needed to transfer some of that to Adam?

Okay. She could do this. She just needed to give it a try. Nothing ventured, nothing gained.

'Put your hands on the stick.'

'You've had all this time to think of something and the best you could come up with was another flying lesson.' He shook his head. 'Man. We've got a long way to go with you, don't we?'

'This is my turf—remember?' She scowled at him. He wasn't making it any easier. 'You have to do as you're told.'

'Bossy can be sexy. That's a start.' He moved back into place and reached his hands out, curling his fingers around the stick with more care than he'd used the first time.

'You have to be quiet so I can concentrate.' She placed her hands over his and adjusted the angle, her body leaning close to his and her breast pressed against his upper arm.

She could feel the heat radiating off him through her clothes, the responding jump of awareness in her pulse. It was just like last time. Except this time it wasn't Adam backing her into a corner and forcing her to feel things she didn't want to feel. This time it was Adam *inviting her* to feel those things, to explore, to take what she wanted…

It was the most erotic thing she'd ever experienced.

Adam's voice was deeper above her head. 'I don't remember being told not to speak…'

'Adam?' She said his name somewhat huskily, then leaned back a little and looked into his eyes, her voice deliberately low as she smiled at him with meaning.

He smiled back at her—that lazily, deliciously sexual, slightly lopsided smile of his. 'Yes?'

'Shut up.' She batted her lashes, beginning to enjoy her position of control over him.

The smile remained, so with a shake of her head Roane went back to checking everything before she removed one hand long enough to reach over to the autopilot. 'You have the stick now. Just keep it even. Now don't move from there. You see this dial?'

She pointed to one and looked at him long enough to smile at his frowning nod. 'That's your horizon. Keep the line straight and we're good. Got it?'

He nodded again.

Okay, so far so good. Leaning back and letting go of his hands, she checked to make sure he was focusing on what he was doing before starting. She damped her lips. She could do this. No matter what the violent thudding of her heart, her dry mouth and her suddenly clammy palms said to the contrary.

Adam had his profile to her, his ridiculously thick lashes flickering as his gaze shifted from the stick to the horizon to the sky and back to the beginning again. So Roane took a deep breath, her voice husky even to her own ears.

'Now I'm going to tell you a few things about the airplane. So listen up.'

He glanced at her with raised eyebrows that furrowed his forehead.

And Roane nodded. 'Yes—the plane.'

When he rolled his eyes the way she normally did Roane chuckled, leaning in so her face was closer to his. 'Focus on what you're doing; feel the vibration of the engine through your hands and underneath your seat…and listen to my voice…'

Adam glanced briefly at her from the corner of his eye and Roane could see the combination of suspicion and curiosity there. She'd sparked his interest, hadn't she? It was quite the confidence booster.

So she kept her voice low and the words slow, not caring if her own rising arousal was showing. 'You are sitting in two million dollars' worth of precision engineering. She's a thing of great beauty and strength and has more than enough under the hood to make an aficionado shudder with pleasure…'

When he glanced at her again she saw the darkening of his eyes. It told her he knew what she was doing—that he could read the subtext where Roane told him about the kind of woman she would dearly love to be. It gave her a sudden rush of adrenalin, so she swiped her tongue over her lips and let her lower lip slide between her teeth. 'A plane like this comes with a beautifully glossy brochure. I read it from cover from cover. Shall I tell you my favorite part?'

He nodded.

'*Anything is possible…*' She breathed the words, her eyelids growing heavy as she inhaled his sensuous scent and continued, 'People are said to reach a meridian in their lives—a time at which their powers and prowess are at their apex. A time at which anything is possible, and all the objects of desire are suddenly within reach.'

When she glanced down she saw his throat convulse, so she kept going. 'It is a height hard-won, and deeply satisfying. A height from which one can see into the light of things...'

Further down she could see that his breathing had changed, his wide chest rising and falling in shallower breaths, so she let herself get lost in her passion for the subject. 'It's how this plane makes me feel when I'm flying. Up here I'm free, I'm exhilarated, I'm *turned on* by it...Every. Single. Time.'

As free and exhilarated and turned on as she was by what she was doing with Adam...

His breathing stilled while Roane resisted the temptation to allow her gaze to slide down to his lap, instead following it back up to the column of his neck where she could see his pulse throbbing temptingly just beneath the collar of his shirt.

'Then we have the stats—' she took a measured breath '—like horsepower...lift...flight speed...*thrust*...'

The last word was whispered and while she stared the throbbing pulse sped up. So before she could talk herself out of it, she pushed her mike back to make room and bent forwards, pressing her lips to the spot.

Adam's low hiss of pleasure thrilled her, a smile forming against his skin as she lifted her hand and set it on his knee. He tensed. She leaned back just enough to be heard in the mike.

'Cruise speed is two hundred and sixty knots...' Another kiss a little further up. 'She can rise to a maximum altitude of thirty thousand feet...'

Impulsively she flicked her tongue out, running the very tip of it over his skin and closing her eyes to savour the combination of warm skin and hint of saltiness on her lips. He was delicious.

Adam let out a low growl.

'You're wondering about the range...' She slid her hand a little higher up his leg, feeling the muscles in his thigh bunch beneath her palm. 'It's got a thirteen hundred kilometer range…over a thousand nautical miles…'

Simultaneously she ran her tongue over the sensitive skin below his ear and slid her hand a little higher up his thigh, his body heat seeping through the material of his jeans and into her palm. 'We could cross the Atlantic with this plane, Adam…'

Then an undiscovered vixen within her asked, 'How long do you think you would need?'

'Roane?' Her name was said on a harsh note.

She moved back enough to be heard and to study a muscle clenching in his jaw. 'Yes?'

'If you keep doing that in about thirty seconds I'm gonna crash this plane.'

'No, you won't.' She smiled drunkenly, intoxicated by his reaction.

'Oh, yes, I will.' A short burst of deep masculine laughter sparkled into the air. 'And when we die I'm gonna haunt you for all eternity.'

'No, you won't.' Roane's smile grew, her gaze tangling with his. 'I'd have had to disengage the autopilot for that to happen…'

Adam frowned. 'You reached over.'

'Mmm-hmm—doesn't mean I did it, though.'

There was a comical moment of uncertainty when Adam frowned harder at the stick in his hands and then back to her, realization narrowing his eyes. 'So if I let go of this thing we won't plummet into the ocean.'

'No plummeting.'

His voice deepened as he loosened his fingers. 'Sweetheart, you're in so much trouble about now it's not even funny…'

'Ah-ah-ah.' She leaned back and waggled a finger at him when he turned her way, joy bubbling effervescently inside her at her achievement. 'No, you don't. You're all mine, remember? Temporary slave. At my command.'

'I'm calling a do-over due to foul play.'

Roane grinned. 'What are you, *seven?* You can't call a do-over. The rules were set before we left the ground.'

'You're a con artist, Elliott.'

'No-oo…it turns out I have hitherto unknown talents… who knew?' She shrugged a shoulder and continued grinning ridiculously as she checked the readouts and how far they were from home. 'I think I might just get to go to the top of the class for this one. Go me.'

When Adam didn't say anything she looked over at him and found him studying her with hooded eyes, the smile he aimed her way enough to melt her into a puddle on the floor. Then his voice rumbled huskily over her headset.

'Two words, little girl…'

Roane lifted a brow.

'Pay…back…'

'That's one word,' she calmly informed him while her body flamed in anticipation.

Adam shook his head as he turned forwards in his seat. 'The amount of it coming your way merits more than the one word.'

It sent a shiver of excitement up Roane's spine. But she'd known what he'd do if she was successful, hadn't she? Maybe it was why she'd put so much effort into it. It had taken very little, surprisingly. Whether that was because his mind had already been engaged on the subject before she'd ever got started or because she'd let him read innuendo where he chose to on an otherwise innocent subject she didn't know.

But the sense of empowerment it engendered in Roane was unparalleled except for the day she'd gained her pilot's licence—and her freedom along with it.

Adam's idea of payback suddenly felt more like a *reward*...

The plane shook a little and Roane disengaged the auto-pilot to begin their decent through the mild turbulence. She glanced at Adam and saw his large hands gathering into fists on his knees again.

'Adam?'

'Mmm-hmm?' He made the sound almost absent-mindedly. As if his mind was already engaged on methods of payback...

'Just out of curiosity...'

The edge to her voice got his full attention. 'Yes?'

Roane noticed he didn't seem bothered by the second bump they hit. 'If I had kept doing what I was doing—just how long *would* you have needed?'

There was a moment of silence—then laughter. The deep, rumbling, very male sound was mesmerizing to Roane. It changed him. Light danced in his eyes, laughter lines made crow's feet at the outside edges of his dense lashes, the deep grooves in his cheeks framed his smile while ridiculously white teeth flashed at her. He was the most gorgeous man she'd ever laid eyes on. And pretty soon he was going to make love to her. She didn't know when or where, her imagination was now having one heck of a time with the how—but it was a certainty, a fait accompli...

Roane had always had very fixed opinions on the idea of falling into bed with a man she didn't know. But it didn't feel wrong to her; she felt as if she'd known Adam a lot longer than she had, that he wouldn't judge her for caving in so easily. With him she felt free in a way she never had before. It was addictive. As if doing away with all the associated un-certainties of dating and building a relationship removed all the pressure at the same time. She could just be herself and consequences be damned. It was a rare form of emancipation.

'You're a very different woman on your own turf. You know that, right?'

Roane thought about that, her voice low. 'I guess. I've never really thought about it before. On the ground I'm... *grounded*...no pun intended.'

When she accompanied the last word with a wry smile Adam smiled devilishly at her. 'Well, then, we'll have to see what we can do about making you soar when you're on terra firma, won't we? 'Cause this version of you? It's *somethin'*...'

It was the nicest compliment anyone had ever paid her, a part of Roane blossoming and growing under the warmth of his praise. And *that* feeling?

That was *somethin'*...

CHAPTER SIX

ADAM WATCHED AS his father considered his chess move. Roane had been right; further into the routine of the day he was vastly more lucid than he'd been the first morning Adam saw him. By late afternoon he was giving Adam a run for his money.

Playing chess was the one thing they'd done that Adam remembered with any degree of fondness. It had been an especially important break during the times when they'd disagreed on pretty much anything and everything else. The arrogance of youth had begun butting heads with the self-perceived wisdom of experience by Adam's early teens…

He sighed lightly—as much at the new perspective on the past as the amount of time the old man was putting into considering his move. Stubborn old bastard. Despite the fact he was much frailer than Adam remembered, the description still held true. Adam had heard the way he talked to the nurse, who obviously had the patience of a saint.

His father reached out a pale-skinned hand and moved his rook. Adam calmly reached out and moved his knight.

The old man frowned. 'Been practising.'

'Every now and again.'

'You always were too smart for me, boy…'

Adam frowned. Where had that come from?

'Your mother was smart. Get it from her. Look like her too.' He smiled down at the board. 'Beautiful woman…'

Adam watched as his father's chin lifted, a look of confusion on his face. 'She here?'

'No, she's not here.' It wasn't the fact the old man was confused enough to ask about the ex-wife who'd died when Adam had been ten that surprised him. It was the fact he looked so stricken when he was told she wasn't. 'It's your move.'

His father looked into the middle distance. 'She never liked the island. Couldn't settle…'

'I know.' Adam's mother had viewed the island as a desert rather than the oasis, especially during the off season.

'Tried. Both tried. Didn't work.'

'I know.'

He looked Adam in the eye. 'She took you away.'

Adam clenched his jaw. 'I visited. You taught me to play chess.'

He smiled wistfully. 'You learned fast. Beat me when you were seven.'

Adam nodded. 'It had patterns I liked. They made sense.'

'Always good with math. Made money that way, didn't you?'

The statement made Adam's eyes narrow. 'How do you know that?'

But his father's attention was waning again, his gaze searching the room. 'Dinner at five.'

When Adam checked his wristwatch and found it was ten to, the nurse magically appeared to announce, 'Mr. Bryant needs to get ready for dinner now.'

'Dinner at five,' his father repeated.

'That's right, Mr. Bryant. Now, let's get you to the table, shall we?' She smiled warmly at Adam. 'Will you be joining your father?'

'No, I have a few calls to make. But I'll come back.' He helped the nurse to get his father to his feet, surprised at how much shorter he was compared to Adam's memories. He'd always remembered Edward Bryant as an imposing bear of a man. 'We have a game to finish.'

His father smiled, lifting a hand to pat Adam's forearm. 'We'll play chess, boy. I'll teach you.'

Adam went for a walk to fill in time. He was restless, and not just because his father was so changed. Feeling restless wasn't anything out of the ordinary for Adam. He got itchy feet several times a year. The difference was he was usually in a position to do something about it. Like visiting one of his projects or driving across country to a different city to see friends or check out something he'd found interesting enough to invest in.

But within a few hours of stepping back onto the island that day he was restless in a way he hadn't been in a long time. The thing was, it had very little to do with the location—if anything he quite enjoyed revisiting some of his favorite places on the estate.

No, this had more to do with the woman who was thousands of feet up in the air taking businessmen to Boston. Something she'd neglected to tell him she was doing until they'd been safely on the tarmac and his thoughts had been focused entirely on a very sensual payback.

So he'd left her with a kiss that had barely scratched the surface of how turned on they both were by the game she'd played in the air. And walking away from her had cost him his first cold shower in...for ever...

When his phone rang he frowned—the sound seemed so out of place where he was. Time for a reality check from his new life, it seemed.

'A.J.—it's Sol.'

Adam's gaze strayed towards the main house as he made his way up the grassy, tree-lined laneway. 'You get the information I wanted?'

'I did. He's been trying to buy up shares for the last eighteen months. But you still hold the majority.'

'Does he know that?'

'Not that I can tell. You're pretty well hidden. You wanted it that way.'

'I still do.' Adam breathed deep. Then he asked the question that had been bugging him for the past half-hour. 'Does anyone else know?'

For a brief second it had felt as if the old man knew what Adam had been doing since he left. It suggested he'd kept tabs on him. But if he had then why had Jake needed to hire people to find him?

'Not unless they've been doing a lot of digging.'

'How would we find that out?' The thought of someone poking their nose in his business irritated the hell out of Adam. He didn't like his privacy invaded. Being judged because of his name had never appealed to him, nor had the associated publicity. His mother had been hounded by scandalmongers until the day she died.

Sol hesitated. 'I honestly don't know.'

Meaning Adam would have to try and find out from the old man—without giving anything away. He didn't want to play his hand yet.

After running through a few things with Sol he made his way back into the house, and found his father asleep. The nurse appeared beside him. 'He gets tired after dinner some-times. He'll nap. I left the pieces on the board if you decide to continue the game.'

Adam nodded, frowning at what could have been an analogy for other things.

'I'm sure he'd like you to stay. He talks about you all the time.'

It was the second time someone had told him that since he came back. It was still hard for Adam to believe. But he nodded and made his way to the end of the room where there were bookcases jam packed with everything from books on economics to the classics. Sitting on an ancient leather chair with a high wing back, he stretched his legs out in front of him, his gaze randomly discovering a pile of old photo albums. There to help jog the old man's memory, most likely.

Lifting one, he opened it.

Roane came into the room so silently he didn't know she was there until his father stirred. 'That you, girl?'

'It's me, Edward.' Her voice was impossibly soft and Adam looked around the edge of his chair to see her bending over to place a kiss on the old man's forehead. 'I've come to read to you.'

'You're a good girl.'

Roane smiled at him, reaching for a book on the night-stand. 'We're still reading Dickens. *Great Expectations,* remember?'

'You weren't here.'

'I know. I'm sorry.' She pulled an armchair over. 'I had to fly to New York. But I'm here now.'

Adam watched as she tucked her hair behind her ear and opened the book, her voice clear and mesmerizingly feminine as she began to read.

It had been a long time, if ever, since a woman had wound

him as tight physically as Roane had and then left him hanging. Adam hadn't liked it. But what he liked even less was the sudden realization that he'd spent the rest of the day thinking about her. She'd been in the back of his mind the whole time—like whispered words just out of earshot. It wasn't supposed to be that way.

His distraction was proving too distracting…

In the soft glow of a reading lamp she was incredibly beautiful. Not in a classical way, not in a supermodel way, but in a completely fresh and…untouched-by-the-world way. She had the same timelessly serene beauty as the island, as if she were a product of her surroundings rather than genetics. In New York he'd told her she should see the world. But Adam had the feeling she would never be quite the same anywhere else. She *belonged* where she was…in the very place Adam never had…

He leaned back into his chair, careful not to let the leather creak. Then he continued to look through the album, watching his early life unfolding until something she was saying caught his attention. Lifting his hand from the album he randomly toyed with one of the thin leather bands on his wrist while he listened to her voice as she read.

That was a memorable day to me, for it made great changes in me. But, it is the same with any life. Imagine one selected day struck out of it, and think how different its course would have been.

Her voice wove as much of a spell over Adam as the words she was quoting.

Pause you who read this…and think for a moment of the long chain of iron or gold, of thorns or flowers, that

would never have bound you, but for the formation of
the first link on one memorable day.

Like when he chose to take a dip in the ocean after a long
drive across country to the stretch of beach he had gone
skinny dipping on countless times in his late teens? Where
Roane had found him; *the first link on one memorable day...*

Adam frowned at the thought. Why did it suddenly feel
more important than it was? He'd never been a romanticist.
His mind wasn't built that way.

'Where's the boy?'

Roane's voice was infinitely patient in reply. 'Adam's not
here. Not right now. But he's home. He came to see you. He'll
come see you again.'

Adam leaned forwards and saw her take his father's hand
in hers, a gentle smile on her lips a she reassured him, 'Really
this time. You didn't imagine it.'

'Gone too long...'

'I know. But he's here now.'

Adam was still coming to terms with the idea of having
been talked about with Roane before he'd even 'met' her—
he wasn't sure how he felt about that—when something
happened that he never thought he'd see: his father began to
silently weep.

His voice cracked on the words, 'Where's the boy, Grace?'

Adam's mother's name...

Roane had to clear her throat. 'He's—'

'Here.' Adam set the album to one side and stood up, his
gaze finding Roane's and noting the surprise in her eyes
before he used the word he hadn't used in a long, long time.
'Dad—I'm right here.'

Still aware of her gaze following his every move he walked

to his father's bedside and placed a hand on his shoulder. A cold hand rose to his, the old man's voice threaded with emotion.

'Sorry, boy. I let you down.'

'It's all right, Dad.' He nodded at Roane's lap. 'Keep reading.'

The even tone was absent from her voice when she started reading again, indicating how unsettled she was by his appearance. So when Adam stepped back and pulled a chair over to sit opposite her he purposefully kept his focus on his father. After a while her tone evened out, taking on the hypnotic edge that eventually lulled his father to sleep.

When it did Adam looked at Roane, her gaze rising from the book to tangle with his. It might only have been seconds they stared at each other, but it felt like longer to Adam. Then they rose at the same time, met at the door, and walked through the house to the outdoors—not talking or touching until they got to where the air felt infinitely lighter than it had before and Adam felt as if he'd shed twenty pounds.

'I didn't know you were there,' she said on the gravelled path to the laneway between the main house and the guest house. 'I'm sorry.'

'How long have you been reading to him?'

'A little over a year; he likes the classics best.'

They stopped in the laneway, the sky a stunning display of ochre and gold over their heads as the day faded. Then Roane turned to face him, her chin rising and the luminous blue of her gaze searching his. 'He really did miss you, Adam. When he's his most confused he gets emotional and says he has to find you to make it right. You're the one thing he left undone. You being here, it means more to him than you realize…'

Adam looked over her head, staring into the distance as

he fought to assimilate the information. The old man was different. Maybe at some point Adam had mentally exaggerated the image with the perceptions of the archetypical angry young man he'd been back then. Maybe it was simply because of the illness he seemed so changed. Adam didn't know. The thing was, they were both stubborn. He was more like his father in that respect than he'd probably ever have admitted.

Roane stepped closer. 'There's still time.'

Adam frowned. He'd thought he had it all planned out. But things were different. He hated the lack of clarity. So much for the plans he'd made...

One small hand lifted to turn his face, her palm sliding upwards to allow her fingers to spread against his cheek. Then she stood on her tiptoes and surprised him by pressing an all too brief kiss to his lips. 'You did good.'

Was she patronizing him? Adam's brows jerked upwards in disbelief. He searched her eyes for confirmation as her hand dropped back to her side. No. She wasn't. She'd been helping to care for his father for at least a year so she knew what worked to soothe him and what didn't. She was simply telling him his words and his tone and his presence had helped...

But somehow knowing that didn't help Adam's mood. In fact if anything it made him angry. He didn't need her to soothe him.

Moving swiftly, his large hands framed her face, fingers thrusting into the soft curtain of her hair as his lips crashed down on hers. She rocked back a step but he didn't make any attempt to support her. Instead he took. He demanded. He devoured and in a heartbeat her whimper of protest morphed into a moan.

Small hands lifted to grasp onto the anchor of his open

shirt. Then she kissed him back, tangling her tongue with his. It was frantic and primal. It was the tension that had been building between them let loose without any hint of coherent thought.

Adam smiled with satisfaction before lifting his head and reaching for her hand. 'Come on.'

Her voice was husky as she let him guide her across the lane. 'Where are we going?'

Adam stopped and turned, towering over her while she looked up at him with eyes darkened several shades by desire. 'Where do you think we're going?'

It took a moment, but then her lips formed an 'o' and her eyes widened, her gaze darting past him to the guest house and then back to his chest. 'I can't…I mean…well, it's just that…'

Adam attempted to read between the lines. 'You're not sure? You're having second thoughts? All of the above?'

'No, well, yes and no…I just…' Indecision shimmered across her eyes and she shifted her weight from one foot to the other before glancing up at him. 'You're gonna think this is pathetic.'

Adam flexed his fingers around hers. 'Try me.'

'It's just that the guest house…'

When she grimaced and waved a hand in the direction of the house behind him Adam had a sudden flash of insight; it was about *location*? The idea made him smile.

His smile made her frown, her hand slipping free from his. 'I told you you'd think it was pathetic.'

Adam forced the smile off his face and folded his arms across his chest while he attempted to keep the amusement from his voice. 'So what's wrong with the guest house exactly? It has five bedrooms—you can take your pick.'

She shot him a scowl before looking at the house again. 'There's nothing wrong with it. It's just it's…well, it's impersonal. Like a really fancy hotel impersonal. And this is already—'

'Impersonal?' Adam's brows rose in surprise. That was how she saw what they were doing? 'There aren't too many things in this world as personal as sex, sweetheart. When you get naked in a bed with someone it's *personal*.'

'With me it is. But you're the guy who gets naked at the drop of a hat.' When Adam angled his head and eyed her with suspicion she clarified what she'd meant. 'I don't need to remind you how we met, do I?'

Roane took a breath and tried again. 'The guest house. Well, maybe it's the word guest. It's not a home, it's impersonal and that makes this, well, it—'

'Cheapens it.' He didn't make it a question.

Roane exhaled her reply as if she was relieved he understood. '*Yes*. I'm sorry. I just don't want it to feel like that…'

It wouldn't. He'd make sure of it. 'So you'd be more comfortable in your own space.'

'Comfortable is possibly a stretch, but yes.'

Adam could feel her nervousness shimmering in the space between them; mixed in with the heat she naturally radiated it formed a tantalizing glimpse of things to come. He knew instinctively she would tremble when he touched her, that the awakening of her body would both frighten and arouse her at the same time. Every bone in his body ached with the need to watch her as it happened, his arms unfolding and hands reaching out to insinuate their way under her jacket the same way they had earlier. With his gaze fixed on hers he set his palms against the curve of her stomach, a smile toying with his mouth as he felt her tremble. Then he splayed his fingers, adding a little pressure as if to help still her inner shaking as he stepped in and lowered his voice to say one word.

'Where?'

Roane stared up at him as if mesmerized, long lashes flickering as she studied each of his eyes in turn. Adam could feel her wavering indecision; the fine line between sensible thought and physical need wobbling like images caught in the heat waves radiating off a road through the desert. She breathed shallow breaths—her soft skin warmed beneath his palms—she damped her lips in preparation for his mouth…

So Adam leaned in and kissed her. Taking his time to soothe and cajole and tempt while hunger spiralled inside him again. Roane fed that burgeoning hunger with calming touches of her velvety soft lips. She made his animalistic instincts growl with tentative strokes of her sweet-tasting tongue. When Adam fought for breath she breathed air into his lungs with whispered sighs, until the kissing became softer and slower still and he could feel something give inside her.

'Where?' He asked the question against her mouth.

'I live in the beach house.'

Silently stepping back, Adam turned, hooking her forefinger over one of his little fingers. But he didn't make an attempt to reach for anything firmer, as if he was aware of how little it would take to change her mind. The touch was tentative, even when they stepped off the end of the wooden walkway onto the deep sand of the beach—it could have been a metaphor for their relationship.

When her finger almost slipped free he hooked the tip of his ring finger to hold on; Roane smiled nervously in response when he glanced her way and a breeze from the ocean whipped tendrils of her hair against her cheeks. God he wanted her. He craved physical closeness with her the same way the incoming tide craved the touch of the shore.

The small beach house caught his gaze when he looked forwards; its pale blue painted boards and white trim were indicative of houses dotted from one end of the Vineyard to the other. And a thought occurred to him. 'You were going there the night you found me?'

She nodded, studying him as she walked as if she was trying to figure something out.

Adam looked back at the house. They were less than fifteen yards from where she lived now—where she slept— from her *bed*. They were getting closer with every step. The thought made Adam's body stiffen painfully in anticipation. Fourteen yards, thirteen, twelve, eleven…

He looked over at her profile and found her staring out to sea, the deep breath she took lifting her breasts. Then she turned her head and looked up at him and out of nowhere Adam heard his own voice.

'Do you trust me?'

The reward for his question was a dazzling smile, one that had him smiling back in an instant. His smile was then rewarded with a gentle nodding of her head. So he let out the breath he hadn't noticed he was holding to say a husky edged, *'Good.'*

He'd needed to know. There was no going back once they got started; Adam knew that. He just needed to know she knew it too. Her open gratitude that he'd taken the time to ask her an added bonus…

When they reached the foot of the wooden steps to her small porch he stepped close and broke the contact of their hands to set his hands on her hips and draw her close.

She slid her arms under his open shirt and around to his back, pressing her breasts against the wall of his chest and sending a jolt of electricity to his groin. Then she kissed the side of his neck the way she had on the plane, igniting remembered sensations to add to the new ones he could feel growing inside him.

Adam growled appreciatively above her head. 'Fond of that spot, aren't you?'

He could feel the smile on his skin. 'Mmm-hmm…am…'

Decision long since made, he started backing her up the steps, his hands sliding under the bottom edge of her jacket to touch warm skin again. 'You've got buckets full of payback coming your way for earlier…'

'I know.' She rained kisses up the column of his neck and mumbled near his ear, 'I've done nothing else but think about that since I left you…'

Every fibre of Adam's physical being throbbed with the need to feel her moist heat surrounding him, to hear the noises she would make as he moved inside her, freeing the sexual being he knew was hidden within. He hadn't lied. He wanted to be the one to teach her what she could feel, what it could be like when that one intangible was there between two adults. For her to understand how rare it was to have that much chemistry from the get-go…

Tightening his fingers, he lifted her off the ground, setting her down on the top step so she was at eye level with him. She lifted her chin and looked deep into his eyes and for a brief second Adam had honestly never felt so naked. Not even when he'd been standing in front of her that first night.

He angled his head and leaned forwards, his mouth hovering over hers as he watched the play of emotions crossing her expressive eyes. One at a time they were easy to decipher. But he had a suspicion the knack of reading them when they were so mixed up was beyond his reach. It would probably take a lifetime to understand the nuances.

But with a complete certainty born of instinct alone he knew that none of them was doubt. She was giving herself to him. It garnered a sense of elation in Adam that made him want to throw his head back and howl in victory.

Instead he leaned over and took his time kissing her, paying particular attention to her lower lip before sweeping his tongue in to taste her addictive sweetness. The second she joined the dance things changed; she kissed him as if she were starving and he were a feast, as if she were dying of thirst and he were a cool drink of water. There was no way Adam could fight it, he couldn't help but devour her right back—because she wasn't the only one who'd been thinking about it all day, was she? He could hear the whisper now, the one that had been in the back of his mind just out of reach—it said her name. As if she was calling to a part of him no one else ever had.

When her hands began to move frantically against his back, reaching under the edge of his T-shirt to touch his skin, Adam tried to find something to focus his mind on; to help slow things down. If he didn't then he knew he would take her. Harder and faster than he knew she was ready for. Later, he promised himself. Not this time. The first time she needed him to exercise some of that control he was usually so good with.

'Adam—' She wrenched her mouth from his to plead breathlessly as he plied kisses to the neck she arched for him. 'Adam, *please*—I want—'

'I know.'

'But I need—'

'I know.'

When he punctuated the words with kisses and nips she shuddered against him. 'You're making me crazy!'

Lifting his head, he smiled down at her. 'Am I now?'

He was glad he was. He wanted her crazy for him.

'Yes.' She frowned. 'I just—I need you to—that is, I want…'

'Tell me.' He looked steadily into her eyes, his voice vibrating low in his chest. 'What you need, what feels good, what you want. Every last request…'

Roane's answer was barely above a whisper. 'I want *you*. I *burn*—for you—you *make me* burn…'

'Door. *Now*.' He kissed her hard, the need to consume her so powerful it took everything he had in him not to rip her clothes from her body.

They practically fell through the door, Adam making a cursory examination of the room before asking the obvious: 'Bedroom?'

Roane walked backwards, mumbling between kisses, 'This. Way.'

Adam reached for the hooks on her jacket, his mouth still fused to hers. It felt like he'd imagined undressing her a thousand times and yet now that he was his fingers were shaking. What was with that? It had been a long time since any woman had made his damn hands shake. It added to his frustration, because their movement coupled with his lack of dexterity meant it took twice as long as it should have to undo the hooks.

Roane removed her mouth from his long enough to look where they were going. While she did the last hook came free, the edges of the jacket opening to reveal smooth, creamy skin only partially covered by deliciously feminine lace. Adam's mouth went dry as he imagined trailing kisses over her skin. He could see her puckered nipples through the thin lace and he swallowed to ease the rawness in his throat.

'You're beautiful.' His voice was gravelly as he slid the jacket off, his thumbs trailing over her shoulders. 'Have I told you that?'

'You haven't.' She looked up at him, her eyes dark in the dying light.

'I should have. You are.' The jacket was tossed aside, Adam's formerly dry mouth watering at the thought of capturing her nipples with his lips. So blinded was he by the thought that he hadn't noticed she was pushing at his shirt until she shoved it off his shoulders and down his upper arms.

'So are you.' She murmured the words in a low, sexy voice that shot another surge of heated blood to Adam's groin. But then the fact she'd divested him of his shirt and reached for his T-shirt—her knuckles grazing his abdomen in the process—probably had just as much to do with it. The thought of her hands on him, around him, squeezing his hard length and guiding him to her—it was almost too much...

'Men aren't beautiful.'

'This one is.' She looked up at him as she lifted his T-shirt.

Adam smiled when she scowled and added, 'You might have to help me with this—you're too tall.'

He yanked it unceremoniously over his head and tossed it in the general direction of her jacket. By then Roane had backed through a doorway and her light summer breeze scent surrounded him, stronger than before. *Her bedroom.* But he didn't look around him beyond discovering the bed, he wasn't the least bit interested in his surroundings—the woman in front of him was all he could see.

She took a shaky breath, he saw her hesitate, and then she reached out a hand. When he dropped his chin he saw her fingers tremble and then they touched, tentatively—like someone holding their hand out to an open flame. Her fingertips traced his chest almost reverently and Adam sucked in a sharp breath, forcing himself to stay still and let her explore.

It was torture.

Groaning low down in his throat with a combination of arousal and a sense of defeat, Adam tried unsuccessfully to find a shred of sanity to cling to. But when she stepped forwards and pressed her lips to a point directly above his heart it was gone in a second; incinerated in the white-hot intensity of one butterfly-soft kiss. She stepped in close, tilted her head back in invitation, so Adam claimed her lips and drank deep.

Lace-covered breasts pressed against his bare chest and he was sweeping his hands up to cup them before he realized he was doing it. On his lips she tasted of sweet, soft woman—on his body her hands splayed across his abdomen, making him suck in a sharp breath that tensed the muscles beneath her fingers. In his hands she was the perfect palm-filling curve he'd known she would be. Thanks to the combination of all those things his jeans were so tight they were painful.

She was killing him. He was *trying* to go slow. But the last vestige of control was slipping fast.

Adam wondered if she was even aware of what she was doing to him. Surely no woman on earth could be so naturally seductive in every way and not be aware of her effect on a man? Each gentle touch of her small, fine-boned fingers, each sweep of her tongue against his, each sigh she made or low hum of approval echoed from her lips to his sent molten fire through him.

Maybe she did know what she was doing to him and was doing it on purpose? He hoped for her sake she wasn't.

Without warning she found the fly of his jeans and cupped his heavy erection. Adam immediately forced himself to pull away, breathing hard from the effort as he gently removed her hand and set her back from him.

'You need to slow down, little girl.'

Roane's voice shook. 'Did I do something wrong?'

'Hell, no.' He set his hands on her shoulders and silently persuaded her to step backwards towards the bed. 'It's what you're doing right.'

The smile was immediate and so bright it lit her up. 'I'm glad. I want to do to you what you do to me.'

'Sweetheart, if you do then my reputation for being any good at this is going to go down in flames.'

'I doubt that.'

Adam scooped her up and laid her down as if she were something infinitely fragile and precious. Then he followed her, his knee dipping the mattress as he lay down beside her and brushed her hair back from her cheek. 'Just let me do all the work the first time.'

Roane's voice came out on a squeak. 'The *first* time? How many times were you planning on there being?'

He smiled a slow smile. 'You thought there'd only be the one?'

'I didn't—I mean I hadn't—I—'

'This isn't a one-time thing.'

She gulped, bringing a wider smile to Adam's face—the combination of seductive siren one minute and nervous innocent the next unbelievably intoxicating.

'Don't hold back, little girl, you hear?'

Roane nodded.

So Adam dipped his head.

CHAPTER SEVEN

'DON'T HOLD BACK, little girl…' Adam had asked Roane in a deep silken tone that wreaked havoc on her nerves.

He had no idea what he was asking of her. But she'd nodded. She wondered if he had any idea how much power he wielded over her. How could he not? He was vastly more experienced and sexually confident than she was…

When he'd kissed her in the laneway with so much pent up emotion let loose it had rocked her to the soles of her feet; literally. She'd panicked when he'd led her towards the guest house, a part of her still recoiling from the idea of sex for sex's sake. But when he'd understood her hesitation there'd been a stronger sense of inevitability that had motivated her to do something she'd never done before. She'd allowed him to take her by the hand and calmly lead her to bed…

Adam slowly lifted his mouth from hers and began to blaze a trail down her neck, the fingers on her stomach splaying and pressing downwards as if staking a claim. *Mine,* that hand said. *Don't move, I'm in charge—I'm going to take you the way you've dreamed I would.*

Roane couldn't seem to find her voice and when she did

all she could do was ask shakily, 'You won't hold back either, right?'

He lifted his head and smiled; a slow, sexy, lopsided smile that sent every nerve in her body humming and created a dull ache in her chest. His fingertips trailed over the curve of her stomach to the button on the waistband of her trousers,

'I don't plan on holding anything back,' he said in a voice as heavenly as velvety smooth dark chocolate.

Roane knew instinctively that he hadn't meant the same thing she had. But that wasn't what they were doing, was it? Holding back physically was very different from holding back emotionally. Perversely, since it was the one thing she'd told herself she didn't want from him—she suddenly felt the loss of the emotion; darned fickle heart.

Adam bent and nuzzled her ear, which did nothing for her control over her vocal cords.

'Trust me,' he murmured huskily, the button on her trousers popping free and the zipper lowering.

His tongue traced the shell of her ear. 'Breathe, little girl…'

Roane exhaled, then inhaled sharply, unaware she'd been holding her breath. That explained the ache in her chest, then. Where had her bravado gone—the unwavering certainty that it was right to let him lead her to where they were? The same inner sense of possible recklessness that had loosened her tongue to tell him she'd done nothing but think about what they were now doing all day long.

Gone the second she'd been struck by the reality of what she was doing, that was where. When she'd feasted her eyes on the perfection of his naked chest again and had felt the same cell-deep need to reach out and touch. She'd faltered then, her physical need for him so strong it had floored her.

That was before she'd brazenly cupped him through his jeans and been momentarily terrified by the logistics of what they were about to do. He was so big. She was so much smaller than him.

She stifled a moan when he ran the tip of his tongue down to the beating pulse at the base of her neck, his hand smoothing her trousers downwards.

'Relax,' he breathed. 'Lift up for me.'

Again she did what she was told, trying her best to relax only to have him move further down the bed when she lifted her hips, making her tremble all over again. When he kissed his way down her shoulder and arm she could have gone limp with relief if his other hand hadn't been sliding up her thigh at the same time.

Then her trousers were gone and he was kissing his way across her collarbone. 'And make noise.' He lifted his head and smiled down at her. 'I want to hear it. Every sigh, every gasp, every moan—let it all out.'

When he lowered his mouth to her other ear a whimper escaped before she could stop it. Between the things his mouth was doing to her ear and where she was afraid his hand was headed—oh, come on, *afraid*? Who was she kidding? *Hopeful* his hand was heading—it was hard to form coherent thought. But she gathered all her will power and tried anyway.

'Do you have—you know? With you?' She heard herself ask the question that could have done with being asked sooner. If she hadn't been half pinned beneath the heavy weight of him she would have kicked herself for not thinking about it before. How stupid was she?

Sleeping with a man within three days of meeting him was insane enough for Roane. Having a baby with him? Beyond insane and into the realms of sheer stupidity...

It didn't explain why her body reacted so strongly to the powerful thought of it, though, did it? For a second she convinced herself she could feel her womb clench.

Adam chuckled, gently nipped her shoulder and Roane jumped, clutching his shoulders as a rush of heat spiralled through her body. But she couldn't stop the disappointment that rose inside her when he pulled back and his hand left her leg.

She'd just messed it up, hadn't she?

When Adam's eyes met hers, he didn't look at her as if she'd ruined everything by bringing up the subject of contraception—or lack thereof. Instead he took her hand and brought it to his lips, turning it over and placing a kiss on her palm before setting it to his chest and sliding it down over his skin. Roane allowed a small moan to escape as she felt the hard muscles under the heated covering of silky smooth skin; it was as addictive the second time as it had been the first. He really was beautiful.

'I have one in my wallet.' He guided her hand over his chest, as if her hand had become an extension of his own. Then he pressed her palm over his heart, on the very spot where she'd kissed him.

'I'll be better prepared next time.' He released her hand and cradled her cheek with what almost felt like tenderness. 'All the more reason to take our time…'

Roane's heart kicked hard against her breastbone when Adam lowered his head and coaxed her lips apart. She slid an arm around his neck, whimpering wantonly when his tongue caressed hers and drew her into a leisurely dance. Frankly she hadn't known what she'd expected of him— heat, passion, fire, strength; all those things and more, yes. During the day she'd mentally toyed with all of the associated images of those things. But the last thing she'd expected from him was tenderness.

He tasted her as if he had all the time in the world and intended to make the most of every single second. Roane had no emotional defence from that, a part of her reaching out for it and trying to clasp it tighter to her fickle heart. Rough-tipped fingers traced her cheek, the arch of her brows, the curve of her lashes when she closed her eyes. Then they threaded into her hair, bending at the knuckle to brush it out into a curtain on the pillow beneath her head.

Roane's hand was still where he'd left it, the beat of his heart reverberating through his skin and into her palm. She felt the rhythm, her heart matching beat for beat when she felt it quicken. Then she slid her hand upwards, over his shoulder, around to his back—suddenly feverish with the need to touch him, to learn every last inch of him as if there would only be the one time for them despite his silken promise.

Adam's muscles jumped as she impulsively trailed her fingernails over his skin. Roane felt a thrill shooting through her at the effect her touch had on him. Had she really done that to a man like him? He drew her closer, his breathing speeding up as the kiss spun endlessly on and on.

With a deft flick of his thumb and forefinger she felt the front clasp of her bra come undone and then a large hand un-erringly found her naked breast making her arch and moan out loud. It was the most intense sensation. His touch sent shivers radiating outwards from her breast to the rest of her body. Then he rolled her nipple in his palm and kissed her again in that slow, relentless tantalization he did so very well.

She began to writhe restlessly against the covers, the hand not clinging to Adam bunching the material into a fist. But Adam simply continued endlessly caressing her and kissing her until she thought she'd explode into a million pieces if he didn't do more.

'*Adam.*' She moaned his name when he pulled back to kiss his way along the line of her jaw.

'I know,' he whispered roughly in reply.

Then he bent and caught her nipple between his lips, drawing it into his mouth and gently grazing it between his teeth. The soft bite effectively short-circuited Roane's brain, the one leg not pinned under the weight of his moving frantically as she grasped the covers tighter and twisted them.

'God—Adam.' Her throat was raw from gasping in air, her heart beating so fast that her chest ached. Down below, dear heaven, she had no idea what that was. It—well, it almost hurt. She was hot and tight and tingly and—

Adam continued to bestow his expertise on her breasts until Roane honestly thought she would die of longing if he didn't touch her lower down. It was too much and not enough at the same time. She had no idea what it was that was happening inside her abdomen or how she was supposed to control it. It was as if every muscle in her body was straining to grasp onto something that was just out of reach. Something her very life depended on.

The hand on his back slid up into his short hair, fumbling blindly for a hold.

He rested his chin on her ribcage, his voice sending a cooling whisper of air over a heated nipple as he made the soft demand: 'Tell me what you want, little girl.'

Lying in bed with him, Roane discovered the nickname took on deeper sexual undertones. She twisted her hips and found the words were easier to say when she craved his touch so very badly. 'Lower. Touch me lower.'

'Here?' His hand slid down over her ribs to her hip.

'Lower.'

The hand moved to her thigh. 'Here?'

Roane frowned at him, her voice strangled. 'You *know* where. You know what you're doing to me. *Please.*' She felt emotion clogging her throat. 'Please don't make me beg you.'

Adam moved back up, resting his head on the pillows beside her and turning her face towards him with one long forefinger. 'Anything you give me you give me freely.'

Roane felt tears welling up in her eyes, her answer an exhaled whisper. 'Thank you.'

He smiled at her in the silvery moonlight, moving his hand down her throat, over her breast, her stomach, her abdomen and then—finally—beneath the band of lace to push it down and away. Roane knew to bend her knees and lift her hips, she knew to wriggle just a little and to hook her toes to slide the lace off her ankles and away. Then Adam's fingertips were moving back up her leg, over the sensitive skin behind her knee, the softest part of her inner thigh—to where she desperately needed his touch the most.

When his fingers dipped into the pool of wet heat she turned her head and arched back into the pillows, her hips rising off the bed as she bit down on her lip.

'You really have been thinking about this all day, haven't you?' he asked with what sounded like a sense of deep satisfaction in his voice.

'Um…' She managed to gasp.

Talented fingers dipped and swirled. 'You've been like this all day. For me.'

Roane gritted her teeth, hissing back, *'Yes.'*

'I wish you could se how beautiful you are right now.' He took a breath. 'Look at me. I want to see you.'

She was focused so intensely on the movement of his

fingers it took him to make the softly spoken demand to her a second time before she turned her head. But having him look into her eyes while he did what he was doing made her feel more vulnerable than she ever had before.

He was studying her intensely as he slid an exploratory finger deep inside her, the question forming in his eyes before he spoke. 'You're tight.'

'Tell me what to do.' She moaned and bared her soul to confess: 'I don't know what to do.'

Adam's thick lashes flickered as he searched her eyes, the question still hovering on his raised brows before he told her in an impossibly tender voice, 'Take a deep breath, relax your body—let the air out of your lungs slow. And. Let. Go.'

She kept looking at him as she followed each step, her body shaking from the inside out as she took a deep shuddering breath, tried with all her might to relax her body and then—

He moved his thumb to her most sensitive spot as she exhaled. He circled, flicked over the swollen nerve ending—and her world fell apart.

Her spine bowed up from the covers, her head pushed deep into the pillows and with her eyes closed tight she could see a myriad of colours flash briefly across her eyelids while she let out a long keening moan. One that seemed to come from the very place he was touching.

Her hips jerked as the waves pulsed outwards. And then after what felt like an eternity she flumped lifelessly against the covers, an almost manic burst of husky laughter escaping from low in her throat. "What the hell was that?"

Adam moved his hand and was brushing his knuckles back and forth over her highly sensitized abdomen, the muscles beneath still jerking with miniature aftershocks when he asked, 'You don't know?'

'I've never. Well, it's just never—' She swallowed to ease her aching throat, then swiped her tongue over dry lips. 'I mean I've tried…I just didn't know…'

Adam's face rose above hers, incredulity in his deep voice. 'What kind of guys have you been with?'

'Ones who didn't know what they were doing.' She laughed again—the sound softer this time. '*Obviously.*'

Adam repeated the word: '*Obviously.*'

Before she could get herself out of a potentially embarrassing conversation he added, 'So that's the first time you've ever—'

'Yes,' she interrupted before he said it, colour rapidly rising on her cheeks. How did she even begin to explain her disastrous love life to a man like Adam? It wasn't as if she hadn't tried, but she'd never felt what he'd just made her feel. 'I think I'd have noticed if *that* happened before.'

Grimacing at how ridiculously shy she suddenly felt, she looked up at him from the corner of her eye. 'That's supposed to happen every time?'

'It is if you're doing it right.' He brushed her hair back from her cheek. 'And that's just the pre-show…'

Roane's breath hitched. 'Pre-show?'

When he kissed her again she was stunned at how fast her body responded even though the heat built slower than before. Somewhere in the midst of roaming touches and gentle sighs and murmurs of encouragement Adam was as naked as she was and Roane was looking up at him as he returned to her having sheathed himself. He kissed her throat, her collarbone, found sensitive places she didn't even know she had, worshipped her breasts until she was writhing against the covers again. She would never have believed a man could master her body the way he was.

Then he smiled at her and kissed her hungrily, his hand sliding down to her waist and over her hip before rising to cup her breast. Any semblance of protection Roane had left shielding her heart melted as he rested his forehead against hers; eyes closed, his skilled fingers tracing the soft mounds of her flesh and his deep voice rumbling into the heavy air with words that surprised her,

'I don't want to seduce you, little girl.'

Roane blinked up at him with wide eyes. He didn't? Had she done something wrong? She wanted him to feel the same way she had, or even a quarter of it. It was only fair. But more than that—she needed him to feel it, to want her beyond reason the way she did him. What would it take to make a man like him feel that way? she silently asked—so desperate for an answer her voice shook.

'You don't?'

Adam opened his eyes and the corner of his sinfully tempting mouth rose in a hint of his devastating lopsided smile. 'Oh, I want you, sweetheart—don't doubt that.'

As if to make sure she got the point, his thumbnail traced a slow circle around her nipple, her entire body tightening in response as he continued speaking in the rough-edged tone that did the most damage to any shred of microscopic resistance she might have had left. 'I want to show you everything you've been missing. I want to be deep inside you. I want to feel you wrapped around me and to hear your moans in my ears. I want to spend days doing this now I know what it feels like.'

The fire in her blood boiled like molten lava at the mental images his words created.

'But?' She choked the word out. 'Cause there was a 'but' in there somewhere, wasn't there?

Adam's hand left her breast and cupped her cheek, his gaze intense. 'I don't want to *seduce* you.'

Reading the confusion on her face, he traced her cheek with infinite tenderness. 'So tell me you want this. No looking back and regretting it. Last chance…'

Roane stared at him, dumbstruck. He was calling a halt to make sure she wasn't swept away by the heat of the moment? He really wanted her to make a rational decision about something as completely irrational as how much she ached for him? How much she'd ached for him since the second she'd laid eyes on him.

'I can't think straight when you kiss me the way you do. Don't you know that?' she whispered, taking the weighty complication of actually choosing to *make love* with him—a phrase so much more dangerous than 'have sex'—out of her hands.

Adam leaned down and grazed his lips over hers. 'You do that to me too.'

Sliding her hands up his muscled arms and over his broad shoulders, she listened to his rasped intake of breath and smiled in amazement. 'Really?'

'Really.'

It made her look beyond her own physical reactions to his. She could feel exactly what she did to him. It was hard, hot and pressed against her hip. But more than that his breathing was ragged, his body was covered in a fine sheen of perspiration, his muscles trembled where she touched—and Roane was shaken by how badly she wanted to keep doing all those things to him.

But only if he would keep doing it back to her…

'*Show me.*' She made the request more confidently, her palms sliding down over his chest and lower still—the need to take him in her hands so strong she shook from head to toe.

With a sudden move that caught her off guard, he removed her hands and pinned them above her head—the submissive position ramping up her desire several notches. He could take her if he wanted to and she knew she wouldn't be able to stop him. Why didn't that scare her the way it should? If anything it made her more excited than she'd been before...

'Say it.'

Removing responsibility from him if she got emotionally involved and had her heart broken the way she inevitably would. Roane bit down on her lower lip and saw his thick lashes lower as he watched the telltale movement.

It was already too late for her. 'Yes.' She had to pause to clear her throat, her heart pounding with a mixture of trepidation and agonizing arousal. 'I want you to make love to me.'

When he lowered his head to kiss her again Roane fully expected ferocity from his kisses as a reaction to her surrender; sizzling fire that would wipe every thought from her mind and make her forget the aching in her chest. But his full lips brushed hers in a feathery caress that both amazed and terrified her.

It wasn't enough, not after he'd made her take complete responsibility for what was about to happen. Her fingers threaded forcefully into his short hair and she bit his lower lip with a growl that stunned even her. Since when had she turned into such a wanton woman in the bedroom? She hadn't known she had it in her.

Adam groaned, his arm tightening into a steel band around her. When he kissed her again she forgot to breathe. Endlessly the kiss went on, his heart pounding heavily against her breasts as her fingers tightened in the soft spikes of his hair. Nothing had ever felt so right in her entire life. Making love with him wasn't a mistake; she knew it with all her heart.

His mouth left hers to blaze a hot path down her throat, making her arch and moan with complete abandon.

'You're so damn beautiful.' Adam mumbled the words before capturing one peaked nipple in his mouth again.

Roane cried out, arching into his mouth as her hands cradled his head to hold him in place. Each flick of his tongue drew another gasp or moan from her. When she dropped her chin to look down at him she was transfixed by the sight of his head bent over her. He had his eyes closed, was making low growling noises that suggested he took as much pleasure from what he was doing as she was receiving. He made her *feel* beautiful. It was the most amazing feeling.

He transferred his attention to her other breast.

Roane had to touch him. So she slid her hands over the back of his head, down the taut line of his neck, skimming across his back while she marvelled at the play of muscles and heated skin slick with a cooling sheen of moisture. Then over his lean hips, up his sides, across his broad chest, back over his shoulders—in a restless, almost frantic exploration that only made her want more of him.

Because he was still holding back. All of his incredible strength of body and spirit held in careful check. Her heart pounded, ached, twisted, she arched upwards with each pull of his hungry lips. Still not enough. *More.* It echoed so deep inside her she thought she might die without it.

Roane moved her hands back to his hair and pulled his head back from her breast, claiming his mouth while revelling in the glorious slide of his body against hers.

He reached down and pushed a long finger inside her, drawing another moan from her that mingled with his groan of frustration. 'You need to relax for me or I'll hurt you.'

'You won't. I know you won't.' She prayed she was right. He was just so big…

When he eased open her legs to form a cradle for himself he shifted over her, leaning his elbows on either side of her head so she could see how much effort it was taking for him to hold back in the straining of his shoulders.

He kissed her long and slow, then rested his forehead on her shoulder and balanced on one arm while he guided himself to her. As he slid forwards the first inch Roane tensed, gasping at how amazing the intimate invasion felt despite the stretching her body had to make to accommodate him.

When she gasped he tensed, his voice rough. 'Relax.'

She took a deep breath and let it go—he slid an inch deeper and froze, staring down into her eyes as if she was the only thing he could see. 'Again.'

Nothing had ever felt as incredible to her as the excruciatingly slow slide of his body into hers. When he slid deeper she struggled for breath. He rocked forwards and the movement drew another gasp from her lips—Adam's head lifting sharply in reply and his large body frozen over hers.

'Did I hurt you?'

'No.' Her voice was breathless. 'Don't stop.'

'You're so damn tight.' His voice was strangled. 'You should have told me—'

'*Please.* Take me, Adam.' She heard the pleading tone to her voice and moaned at how desperate she sounded. 'You were right about my fantasy. I want you to take me.'

To make her point she pushed her heels into the mattress and lifted her hips, forcing him deeper, a low moan leaving her lips. It was apparently all the proof he needed to slide home in one sharp thrust, both of them moaning in unison when his pelvis hit hers.

Adam kissed her again, his mouth claiming hers and drinking deep as he started to move. It was making love in the truest sense and Roane felt the difference with each and every touch, emotion rising up inside her and spilling out of the corners of her eyes before she knew it was happening.

But by then all she could do was hang on tight to him as he rode her hard and slow, then harder and faster—as if he couldn't stop himself; each deep thrust drawing her closer and closer to the same ecstasy he'd already given her. He didn't release her lips, taking her cries and feeding her his groans. Only when the universe exploded around her again—even stronger than it had before—did Roane tear her lips away to cry out his name with the sheer unmitigated joy of how it felt.

Adam's shuddering groan was muffled in her shoulder, his body statue-still for a long moment as he pulsed inside her. Then he collapsed on her. For a long while he stayed there, dragging deep breaths of air into his lungs while Roane fought to control the hot tears streaming from the corners of her eyes into her hair.

He must have felt the change in her, because his head lifted and his gaze searched her face.

'Are you okay?'

God, why was he so obsessed with the idea of hurting her? She allowed a sob to break free since it was pointless trying to hide it when he already knew she was crying. 'Yes. I just. I had no idea.'

She sobbed again and smiled tremulously at him, letting the tears fall unhindered. 'I didn't know it could be like that. Why didn't I know?'

One large hand cradled her cheek, his thumb brushing the tears away as he rumbled his reply. 'Because it's not always like that. I told you this was rare.'

Had he? Roane didn't remember. But being told didn't make her feel any better. If anything it was worse. What if it never happened to her again? What if Adam was the only one who could make her feel that way? How could she ever have a relationship with someone else and not feel as if something was missing?

Dear Lord. What had she done?

Was love enough on its own without this? Because with Adam there was this but there could never be love. He wouldn't stay—he didn't have it in him. He was as free on the ground as she was in the air. But she was only capable of that freedom because she was grounded. She knew where she belonged in the world, where she was happiest. It was on the Vineyard. The one place Adam had left behind him twelve years ago and had never once been tempted to revisit. There was no future in Adam. Not for her. But she'd known that when she made the decision to sleep with him, hadn't she?

So why did it hurt so much?

She turned her face towards his shoulder and let the first racking sob loose. Adam shifted his weight, circling his arms around her and drawing her close.

'Come here.'

Roane curled into him, her arm tight around his lean waist as she tried to get closer still, as if she could draw from the strength of his body and make it hers…

She felt his lips press against her hair. 'I've got you.'

It was the very thing that scared her most.

CHAPTER EIGHT

SHE SOBBED IT out, then quieted and finally fell asleep in his arms. Adam couldn't remember anything ever affecting him the way those tears did.

He seriously contemplated hunting down the guy who'd left her feeling less than she should after she'd trusted her body to him. He doubted there was more than one given her level of inexperience. Not that he'd managed to complete the act—at least not properly—Adam knew that now. A man who left a woman feeling as unfulfilled as she'd been deserved at least one well-aimed swing, Adam felt.

One of the driftwood logs he'd found on the shoreline crackled and spat sparks into the air. When Roane had fallen asleep he'd slept with her, lulled into the kind of peaceful, dreamless slumber he hadn't experienced in well over a decade. But when he woke up a couple of hours before dawn he gently extricated himself from her and went for a walk to clear his head. Not that he was leaving her. He knew he didn't want her to wake up and feel as if it had been a one-night stand to him. She was worth more. And Adam was nowhere near done with her. If anything he'd only got started.

So he walked the beach the way he used to when his insomnia first started at nineteen, randomly collecting pieces of driftwood that eventually became a big enough pile to make a fire near the rocks outside her house. Sitting on the soft sand staring into the flames was as good a place as any to figure out what had happened. And what he was supposed to do about it…if anything…

At thirty-three he'd had his fair share of great sex. Not that he was promiscuous—only a fool would be in the age they lived in and Adam was no fool—but then neither was he anything resembling a saint. But he'd never had an experience that lived up to the description of making love quite the way it had with Roane either. He'd never been a woman's first lover the way he knew he was for her. It brought out a possessive streak in him a mile wide…

The thought of being the one to show her all she could feel only to walk away left him feeling ridiculously angry. But it wasn't as if he could stay. Thing was, if what had happened was difficult for Adam to understand with experience, then how overwhelming must it have been for Roane with virtually none?

She was just so very—delicate. Not in a weak way. He smiled as he thought about how sassy she could be when riled. Nope, definitely not weak—delicate and soft and innately feminine; all things he found incredibly sensual. When she let down her guard and Adam saw glimpses of the passionate woman inside it enthralled him. He wanted to know everything about her. He wanted to step into her head and see the world through her eyes. He wanted to discover all her secrets, was hungry to learn it *all*.

Maybe that was part of what happened? She'd engaged his mind in a way no other woman had. Like a puzzle he had to unravel. By doing so she'd intensified his physical reaction to her. That made sense to him.

Then there was the way she'd looked him in the eye and told him she trusted him. *'You won't. I know you won't,'* she'd said when he'd told her he'd hurt her if she didn't relax. So much faith in a man she didn't know. So much belief in him. Maybe that was part of it?

After a long time spent staring alternately into dancing flames or out over the ocean, Adam finally had to admit that part of his frustration lay in the inevitability of hurting her *emotionally*. He would. He knew that now and was regretting it in advance.

'Nickel for them…'

Adam jerked his head up and found her standing a few feet away. She'd dressed in a long white nightdress with a soft-looking cowl-necked sweater on top, long sleeves hanging below her wrists. She was ghost-like, surreal and so beautiful she made him ache to have her again. And that was rare too. Usually taking what he wanted was enough to dull the need in him. But he wanted her bad; again and again until the need was dulled if that was how it had to be… He didn't care how many times it took.

He held out an arm. She stepped forwards and accepted the silent invitation, sliding her smaller hand into his. Then Adam leaned back against the rocks and settled her across his lap; circling her with his arms. She leaned her cheek against his shoulder as if she'd done it hundreds of times, tilting her chin up so she could examine his face.

'Couldn't sleep?'

Adam looked down at her without lowering his chin, 'You thought I'd left.'

He didn't make it a question and she acknowledged the fact by nodding. 'I did until I saw the fire.'

'What woke you?'

'I got cold—I don't usually sleep naked.'

'You should stay naked all the time.'

'Not really an option.'

'Pity.'

When he moved a hand to her thigh her fingers toyed idly with one of the leather bands on his wrist. 'What woke you?'

He shrugged, his gaze travelling to the ocean. 'I don't sleep so good. I haven't in a long time.' He glanced down at the top of her head. 'Active mind.'

'Ah.' She nodded. 'It wasn't that I didn't do a good enough job of tiring you out, then.'

'No.' But he knew she needed the reassurance so he added, 'I slept six hours. That's a record.'

'I'm glad.' Leaning back against the support of his arm, she looked up at him with sparkling eyes.

Adam studied her face for a moment before looking back out to sea again. He felt her gaze on him and then she snuggled into his shoulder and took a deep breath. 'I love the ocean. It's good for the soul.'

Something they agreed on, Adam silently admitted, especially when it came to the stretch of ocean they were looking at. When he'd been his most troubled he would sit on the sand while he thought things through. When he'd first been sent to live with his father, new stepmom and half-brother it had been his hideaway. It still had the ability to calm him, even now, his mind wandering to details the way it so often did.

'You know the Indians called the island *Noepe*? It means "Amid the waters." Something to do with the conflicting tidal currents they could see offshore. It wasn't till the English got here that it was called Martha's Vineyard…'

Her head nodded against his shoulder and he heard the smile in her voice while her fingers continued to play at his wrist. 'I did know that. I even have a quote about the island for you to add to your collection.'

'Go on.'

'"Everything that ever happened on earth has happened on the Vineyard at least once. And some things twice…"'

'Who said it?'

'Haven't a clue.' The leather she'd been toying with caught her attention. 'Are these friendship bracelets?'

'That's what some people call them, yes.'

'You have friends?'

Adam briefly squeezed his arms in warning. 'Very funny. They're from people I know in New Orleans. We worked together on a rebuilding project.'

The words brought her chin up, her gaze flickering over his face. 'You stayed after Katrina?'

Adam nodded. 'Lots of folks did. I still go back. Coming through something like that ties you together in a way nothing else can.'

'Were you hurt?' The fine arch of her brows wavered on the question so he could see her concern.

It lowered his voice to a deep rumble. 'I was one of the lucky ones.'

Nodding, she dropped her chin, her gaze falling on a spot at the base of his throat and her hand lifting from his wrist to capture what she saw. 'What are these?'

'Which one are you looking at?' There were two on the thin strip of leather fastened around his neck.

Roane turned it towards the firelight. 'It looks like a little tooth on a blue stone in—pewter maybe?'

'Silver. A shark's tooth.' He smiled with meaning when

she glanced up at him from beneath long lashes. 'For strength and stamina…'

She rolled her eyes, her fingers moving to the second one. 'And this? It's beautiful.'

He felt her turning it over to look at each side in turn. And he knew what she was seeing; antique silver—one side set with an eight-pointed star, the other with an intricate pattern of interweaving circles.

'Open it,' he told her.

'It opens?' She was already lifting her other hand and when it opened Adam could hear the surprised delight in her voice. 'It's a compass—a perfect little miniature compass. Where did you get this?'

He'd thought the pilot in her might appreciate it. 'It was my great-grandfather's—on my mother's side. He was a schooner captain, sailed up and down the coast for most of his life when the Vineyard was still a busy harbour. As the second son he could do what he wanted until his brother died and he had to give it up.'

While he explained the history behind it Roane moved her head, leaning back against his arm and looking up at him with a curious expression. 'Are you making this up?'

Adam lifted a brow. 'Do I strike you as a big fan of fairy stories?'

She crinkled her nose. 'Not so much.'

'Well, then.' He looked out to sea, the sky on the horizon hinting at fingers of amber morning light while he contemplated how far to go with the story of the compass. With a deep breath, he looked down at her from the corner of his eye. 'Wanna hear the rest?'

There was a chance she might read more into it than was there, but she'd trusted him so Adam could trust her in return.

The boundaries of their relationship had already been set, she knew where she stood. Somehow he knew she'd appreciate the story, even before she nodded with enthusiasm.

When she batted her lashes at him he shook his head. 'There's no once upon a time so don't get too excited.'

'Spoilsport.' She pouted.

Adam smiled at her antics. 'He gave it to my great-grandmother as a wedding present. Every time he went to sea she would put it around his neck. So he could find his way back to her, she'd say. Then when he came home he'd put it back round her neck because—'

'Because he'd found his way home…'

When Adam looked down at her she was staring at the compass, a wistful expression on her face. He frowned. Women tended to read between the lines. But before he could backtrack any she closed it over and let it go, leaning back against his shoulder. 'Sounds like they were very much in love.'

They'd certainly been devoted to each other their entire lives; they died within a week of each other he'd been told. But he didn't tell her that. Instead he told her another part of it. 'He found a poem with a compass in it—part of it was engraved on their tombstone here on the island. Smart guy, my great-grandfather—knew how to wrap a woman round his little finger with words.'

Roane snorted gracefully, her fingers playing on his wrist again. 'I bet she let him think he did. What was the poem?'

'Shakespeare.'

She echoed his earlier demand. 'Go on.'

When he hesitated she looked up at him and he saw the flash of realization in her eyes, swiftly followed by what looked like amusement to him. 'I'm not gonna end up wrapped round your little finger with words, Adam.'

'Ah, but I already found a way of wrapping you round my little finger *without words,* didn't I?'

Her chin dropped and she ran her hand down his wrist to his finger. 'Tell me about the ring, then. I'm guessing there's a story to go with it if everything else you wear has one…'

The story behind the ring was out of bounds, especially to her. He didn't need her pity. So Adam pushed his hand underneath her thigh, out of reach; gaining a shudder of awareness from her when he spread his fingers and kneaded her soft skin through the light material of her nightdress.

'It's a famous love poem.'

'The story behind the ring?'

'The Shakespeare.' He looked out at the ocean and smiled, nudging her with the arm supporting her to get her attention. 'Sun's coming up. Look.'

She turned her head, so he shifted her round a little to see better, lowering his mouth to just above her ear to tell her, 'Sunrises fall into the unforgettable experiences category.'

'I know.' Her tone had softened again.

Adam breathed in her light scent—moving his chin against the neck of her sweater to press his mouth against the sensitive skin below her ear. 'Let's see what we can do to make it more unforgettable, shall we?'

'Hmm.' She angled her head to make room for him.

When her hand slid up the inside of his leg Adam felt the rush of adrenalin through his veins. Shifting his hand from her thigh to underneath the edge of her sweater, he sought out her breast, filling his palm. She sank into him in response, her nipple beading as he rolled it; she was so responsive it was becoming a drug to him.

When he lifted his lashes he saw the fiery ball of the sun breaking the horizon.

'I don't remember all of it—' he didn't care if she knew it was a lie '—but it starts with: "Love is not love which alters when it alteration finds" and then moves on to say something about "it is an ever-fixed mark…"'

She turned her face and looked up at him while he looked back at her and continued lightly caressing her breast as he added, 'The bit about the compass is further in…'

Roane searched each of his eyes in turn, her breathing becoming shallow. Then she shrugged back her sleeve and curled a hand around his neck to draw his mouth down to hers. 'No wonder she wanted him to come back to her.'

Adam resisted the last inch that stood between their lips, his gaze locked with hers and his voice a husky rumble. 'Handsome devil too.'

Roane's eyes smiled at him. 'Just would be.'

'Probably a girl in every port…'

He leaned in and brushed her lips with his. Roane in turn lifted her other arm and wrapped it around his neck, light now dancing in her darkening eyes as her voice took on a seductive huskiness.

'Don't ruin it for me.'

Adam studied her eyes and then asked what he'd been burning to know for hours, his voice low and rough. 'Why didn't you tell me?'

'Tell you what?'

'How inexperienced you were.'

When doubt crossed her eyes and she avoided his gaze he leaned back a little, his voice firmer. 'Look at me.'

Her lashes lifted, blinking slowly as she looked into his eyes. Then she took a deep breath. 'Would it have made a difference?'

'No.' Adam tightened his hand against her breast, brushing

his thumb over her nipple and earning a gasp from her parted lips as her eyelids grew heavy. Smiling with satisfaction, he kept his tone deliberately low. 'You thought it would?'

Roane didn't answer him.

Moving his hand, he caught her nipple between his thumb and forefinger, the move arching her spine away from the band of his arm and drawing a soft moan from low in her throat. 'It wouldn't. You've got fire in you. I could see it. Wanted it. Still do.'

'You put the fire in me,' she breathed.

'No. You already had it in you. You just make me want to bring it out. If you tried holding it back I'd work harder for it.' Any man who considered himself a man would do the same in Adam's opinion.

Roane was looking at him as if she'd never seen him before or as if he was something completely new and fascinating to her. It was momentarily unsettling. So Adam moved his hand over her breast again and smiled when her eyes closed and she offered her neck to him.

Tilting his head to one side, he lowered his mouth to her skin and kissed his way up to her ear. 'Ever make love outdoors?'

She groaned. 'We can't.'

He was already moving his hand down her body and dragging her nightdress up her legs. 'Yes, we can.'

'No, we can't.' Her body made a lie of the words by parting her legs as he trailed his forefinger up the inside of her thigh. 'We don't have anything…'

Adam lifted his head to look down at her languid eyes, her full lips parted and waiting. 'Still have a lot to learn, don't you?'

He began lowering her to the blanket he'd brought down

from a swing seat on her porch. When she was lying on her back looking up at him he studied her face, temporarily floored by what he could see in her eyes. She was giving herself to him openly and completely. Even when the flicker of her lashes told him how unsure she was of herself. He brushed her hair back from each of her cheeks in turn, savouring the feel of her soft skin beneath his fingertips. Then he traced her mouth, his gaze lowering to watch as her lips parted and the brush of her exhaled breath whispered warmth over the back of his hand. When he looked back up there was wonder in her eyes too, a sense of awe that he could make her feel what she felt? She really had no idea how much of a siren was buried beneath her cloak of inexperience.

Adam wanted to strip that cloak away and let the siren out to play. He was going to tempt her out...

So he lowered his mouth to hers and sipped from her lips, as if she were the finest of wines and every single drop were nectar. He felt her small, cool hand against his cheek, her fingers splaying out against the skin warmed by the heat of the fire in front of them and between them. When he lifted his mouth he turned his head and kissed her palm, framing the back of her hand with his and threading his fingers through hers as he angled it back and kissed the beating pulse at her wrist before gradually working his way up her arm.

Lifting their joined hands above her head, he got to a point where her sleeve was in the way.

'I told you, you should stay naked,' he complained. 'Up.'

Tugging the sweater unceremoniously over her head, he smiled a small smile at her rumpled hair and shining eyes, balling the soft material in his fist and setting it under her head for a pillow. 'There.'

Gaze locked on hers, he unbuttoned the pearl beads down

the front of her nightdress, his palm pushing the edges apart so he could look at her. Adam had always had a deep and abiding appreciation of the female form, but with Roane it was more than that. He ran his fingertips from the base of her neck, through the valley of her breasts to the indentation on the slight curve of her stomach. She was perfection.

When she shivered he looked into her eyes. Was she cold? No, not cold. He'd made her shiver with desire. *For him.* It made him feel like a god.

Moving his flattened palm, he cradled her hip as he kissed her again; drinking deeper, suckling on her bottom lip until she opened her mouth on a sigh. When he moved his palm upwards, letting it learn the inward curve of her waist, she shifted on the blanket to get closer. But when he let his fingertips whisper over her ribs she squirmed, and he felt the low echo of muffled laughter in her throat. Ticklish. He smiled against her mouth. He liked that.

Kissing her deeper still, he sought out her tongue. Then he filled his hand with her breast again, growling at how perfect a fit she was, the bead of her nipple dead centre in his palm. As if she were made for him, or born from his imagination.

Moving over her and settling into the cradle she'd formed for him he dragged his mouth from hers and kissed down her neck, feeling her arch up into him as he kissed his way to her breast and held it up in his hand to draw her nipple into his mouth. She moaned—and when he caught it between his teeth, she gasped. Adam felt like a musician playing a delicately strung instrument. Each place he kissed brought forth a different sound that then vibrated through him and echoed in empty spaces he hadn't known he had. And when he did know, it felt as if the hollowness had to be filled with her.

Pushing an arm under the upward curve of her spine, he dragged her upright, rocking back on his bent knees and hauling her onto his lap. When he looked up at her he saw wide eyes filled with a combination of arousal and surprise, so he yanked her closer; the material of her nightdress bunched tight between her legs as she came into contact with the ridge of his erection.

Awareness flushed her cheeks. She rocked her hips experimentally against him, her sharp intake of breath and the way she bit down on her lower lip distracting Adam from the rush of blood to his throbbing groin.

'Adam—'

When she breathed his name like that it did him in. Didn't she know that?

Thrusting his fingers into her hair, he angled her head back, using the arm around her waist to control the backward arch of her body as he lowered his head to her breasts. Every pull of his hungry lips earned him another rock of her hips against him, her hands clinging to his shoulders and her fingernails pushing into his skin. He could almost feel the siren struggling free...

He pushed the material off her shoulders, down her arms, letting it pool around her waist as he twisted it around his fist behind her back and pulled it tighter between her legs, adding to the friction of her movement. But when she realized what he'd done she froze, her body trembling from within.

Adam kissed her neck and turned his head to whisper roughly into her ear, 'Don't stop.'

Sliding his hand down, he cupped the back of her neck between long fingers and his thumb and lifted his head—the tip of his nose almost touching hers as he looked into her eyes and tugged the material tight again. 'Take what you need from me.'

Roane swallowed hard, her voice husky. 'I can't.'

'Yes, you can.'

'But you won't—'

'Not this time.' And if she had any idea what it was costing him she wouldn't look at him the way she was. 'I want to watch you.'

'I can't.' The agony in her eyes came through in the wobble of her soft voice. She wanted to please him. What she didn't know was her pleasure alone pleased him. He could wait. For now…

'You can.' He angled his head, his mouth hovering over hers. 'I can make you.'

Still looking into her eyes, he dragged her lower lip between his teeth and let go. 'I can wind you up so tight you won't be able to stop yourself. Your body belongs to me now.'

He kissed the lip he'd tugged when a flash of fear crossed her expressive eyes. 'I can make you do it with words alone if I want to…'

Moving his head again, he set his cheek to hers and spoke into her ear again, his voice low and even, the words purposefully slow. 'I can tell you what it felt like when I was deep inside you. I can tell you what it was like when you came around me…'

Her hips moved restlessly against him, her breathing ragged in his ear.

'I can tell you how amazing it was.' He pressed his lips to her ear lobe. 'I can tell you how much I want to feel it again. And again. And again. I can tell you how many times I want to come inside you the way I did…'

Roane whimpered and moved rhythmically against him.

Adam smiled, holding the material in place and feeling the shudder of her body as she got closer to the edge. 'Take what you need. I want you to.'

'Oh, God—'

She wrapped her arms around his neck and held onto him as if her life depended on it, her breasts rubbing against the wall of his chest and making him wish his T-shirt wasn't in the way. He wanted her skin to skin with him, nothing between them, nothing in the way. He wanted to drive deep into her body and get lost in her. He wanted her screaming his name. He *wanted*.

He was consumed with need. He'd never felt that before. She was like a fever in his blood.

She rocked her hips forwards, grinding herself onto his erection. Then she stilled. A low moan pushed upwards from inside as her body shook uncontrollably.

Adam leaned back, his fingers in her hair so he could pull her head back and see her face. Her eyes were hooded, glittering and so very dark it was almost as if she wasn't there. Her lips were parted, the air she dragged into her lungs making her lower lip tremble. Her cheeks were flushed—a strand of hair was stuck against her damp forehead...

She was *sensational*.

Adam's heart thundered in his chest, his breathing ragged, his gaze so intensely focused on her he was frowning in concentration. He *burned* for her.

Her breasts heaving between them, Roane's eyes slowly returned to a closer shade of the luminous blue he knew so well. She damped her lips, dropped her gaze to his mouth, and then leaned forwards—the voice of a seductive siren making a determined demand: *'Now you.'*

Adam groaned as their mouths fused together. *Hell, yes.* She could do what she wanted. He was all hers.

CHAPTER NINE

WHEN HE TOSSED the helmet at her she scrambled to catch it and looked up at him with wide eyes, laughing nervously. 'Oh, I don't think so.'

'Trust me, sweetheart. You'll love it.'

Her gaze shifted to the shining black metal of his beast of a motorcycle, then back to Adam. She didn't know which one gave her more of a kick to look at, frankly. The motorcycle was dangerous and risky and would probably be the experience of a lifetime—and Adam... Actually in fairness there was very little difference between them. She liked to think Adam was less likely to kill her, though...

He was buttoning up his trademark shirt-worn-over-T-shirt, long fingers moving with the same dexterity he'd used on her body for hours on end. Roane felt a newly familiar rush of heat prickle over her skin as she watched him. How could she still want him that much when he'd pretty much pleasured her into a languid puddle? She had muscles that ached in places she hadn't even known she had muscles, but since each and every ache came with a memory...

On second thought maybe he did have the means to kill her. *But what a way to go.*

He patted the seat of the bike. 'C'mon.'

Roane wavered, grimacing. 'Do I have to?'

The hesitation seemed to surprise him. 'You can fly a plane but you're afraid to get on a motorcycle?'

Cocking a brow, she made a circle with a limp-wristed hand. 'Do we want to turn that one round and take another look at it? Planes are statistically safer than motorcycles.'

He took a long stride towards her and grabbed her elbow, tugging her forwards. 'Have you ever even been on a motorcycle?'

'No. I don't know anyone who owns one.'

'You do now.' He lifted the helmet out of her hands and set it on the seat beside his before reaching out to button up her jacket. 'Consider it one of many firsts I've brought your way. I'm broadening your horizons.'

Roane found it difficult to focus on excuses when the backs of his fingers were working their way up from her stomach, over her ribs and lingering on her breasts. But when he lifted his chin and smiled lazily at her she sighed heavily, fully aware of the fact he knew what he'd just done to her.

'If you kill me I'm never speaking to you again.'

'I'll keep that in mind.' He placed a swift kiss on her mouth and reached for the helmet.

'Please do.' She laughed. ''Cause I'm not much use to you if—' The rest of the sentence was muffled as he pushed the helmet onto her head, patting the top of it with a grin when she scowled at him.

'There.' He buckled the strap under her chin while she set her hands on her hips. 'You're good to go.'

Roane tugged the front of it down a little to tell him, 'You white-knuckle me and this is gonna be the shortest relationship in the history of mankind.'

With a low chuckle, Adam turned and lifted his helmet before casually swinging a long jean-clad leg over the heavy duty touring bike with ease. He then kicked the stand back and lifted it upright as if it weighed as much as a feather— which Roane seriously doubted. She briefly wondered why it was he looked so damn good on it while she was standing feeling like a complete idiot. There was just something about a sexy male on a large motorcycle, wasn't there?

He held out an arm. 'Climb on.'

'I bet you say that to all the girls,' Roane mumbled as she attempted to do as she was told. She wasn't nearly as graceful as he'd been. In fact it took a couple of attempts and some bouncing around on one foot as she tried to keep her balance. All of which Adam found highly amusing, his sensational eyes sparkling at her when he looked over his shoulder.

'Put your feet up. That's it. Arms round my waist.'

All right, so there were certain fringe benefits. Roane was revelling in the sensations of her hips wrapped around his and her breasts pressed tight to the hard wall of his back when he gunned the engine.

Dear Lord. They could just stay where they were. She closed her eyes and let out a low moan she knew he wouldn't hear over the loud rumbling purr of the engine. The vibration sent a rhythmical pulse through the seat to her rear, making her squirm her crotch tighter to the seams of her jeans. She smoothed her hands over his taut stomach, squooshed her breasts tighter to his back so she could feel the heat of him through their clothes… Oh, yes…now this was suddenly *very* interesting.

Adam's head turned and she smiled as he raised his voice above the noise. *'Behave.'*

Roane smiled impishly. She was enjoying her personal

sexual revolution. Now that she knew what she'd been missing out on she was determined to enjoy every single second of it. She wasn't even going to allow herself to think about how brief a time it might be with Adam. All that mattered was the here and now.

When the bike moved smoothly forwards she clung to him, stomach lurching and heart pounding. They bumped cautiously down the laneway, onto the narrow tree-lined road, and when they hit the better surfaces she started to relax. Okay. This wasn't so bad.

She knew he was going slower than he probably did normally but she appreciated the thoughtfulness. He wouldn't let any harm come to her. She knew that. It was the same blind faith she'd had in him when he'd made love to her—she knew he wouldn't hurt her. Oh, he might be rough-edged, but Adam Bryant had an honourable streak underneath it all, didn't he? It added to his overwhelming maleness, Roane felt—was a potent combination when added to everything else.

Women fell for men like him.

The worrying thought made her focus her mind elsewhere, her gaze taking in her surroundings from a totally new perspective. She'd driven along the Vineyard's roads a million times, in a station wagon, as a passenger in Jake's convertible, in her own little compact. But the view from a motorcycle was so very different. She felt closer to nature somehow; a cooling breeze on her face, the scent of freshly mown grass and the salt sea air in her nostrils, the sunlight that danced through gaps in the foliage of the trees creating an arch above their heads. It was glorious.

Then the trees gave way to the ocean, white foam randomly appearing to froth towards the pale sands of the pristine shoreline. Roane held onto Adam's strength to lean back a little so she could smile up at the blue skies.

He threw a smile over his shoulder and she laughed. He'd known she would love this because he knew how it felt. She wondered if he ever got tired of knowing her better than she apparently knew herself. But at the same time she wished she could share her joy of flying with him the same way he was sharing the joy of his freedom on a motorcycle.

It felt as if she was getting more from him than he was from her. Which begged the question of just what it was he got from being with her beyond sex?

By lunchtime they ended up in Vineyard Haven. The boat-filled harbour protected by East and West Chop, promontories that formed a natural enclosure for one of the busiest harbours in the heydays of coastal schooners. It made Roane wonder if Adam's great-grandfather had sailed his schooner from there, with the compass around his neck and his wife waving him goodbye. She smiled at the thought. Then felt an ache at how far back Adam's connections to the Vineyard went. It was sad, especially when he'd left it all behind without a backward glance.

They drove past schooner captains' houses with their bright white porches and heavily laden planters and hanging baskets, then along the tree-lined main street where Adam parked and held out a hand to help her down. Roane was fussing with her hair after removing her helmet when he took her hand.

'Hungry?'

She threaded her fingers with his and smiled at the fact he was holding her hand. Pleasure in the simple things, she supposed. *More to do with the man attached to the hand,* her inner voice admitted.

'Starving.'

'We'll get it to go. Eat at one of the lighthouses.'

When most of the staff in the small general store greeted her by name Adam shook his head. 'I had no idea you were famous.'

'Not famous. *Friendly.*' She adjusted the basket on her arm and scanned the shelves for fresh rolls, smiling as she added, 'You should try it some time. When you first meet someone you can be…surly.'

'Surly.'

'Uh-huh.' She found rolls and moved down the aisle, cocking her head and looking up at him from the corner of her eye. 'And brusque.'

'Surly and brusque.' He looked back at her the same way, then smiled cockily. 'And adorable. You forgot to add adorable.'

Roane snorted. 'It wasn't high on my list.'

Something caught Adam's attention and he set his hands on her hips to turn her. 'That's right. You didn't like me. I'd forgotten.'

'It's been four days. How did you forget that fast?'

'You did. You like me now.'

Good point. Because, darn it, despite the danger she did like him. She more than liked him. It would be so much easier if she didn't…

She searched the shelves to see what he was so interested in. 'What are we—? *Oh.*'

'Ladies' choice.' Leaning down to lower his voice to a deep rumble, he added, 'Just make sure we have plenty. Think strength and stamina…'

He had the gall to slap her rear—firmly—making her jump and scowl at him as he walked away. 'Where are you going?'

Turning on his heel, he walked backwards. 'The produce section. Gotta keep our energy levels up.' He grinned broadly and winked at her. 'Meet you at the checkout.'

Smiling, Roane shook her head, then looked back at the baffling array of contraceptives in front of her. It wasn't something she'd ever spent a whole heap of time looking at in a store. She really wasn't sure she knew where to begin. A ring caught her attention and she lifted it to figure out what it was—swiftly setting it back down when she read the back. It was official—she was a prude. The thought made her frown.

Then she considered the possibilities of some of the items in front of her and felt the heat rise in her body. It was because every image involved Adam. He'd turned her from a prude into a sex maniac in one night.

She glanced up and down the aisle and smiled weakly at someone she knew. Nope. Still a bit of a prude. But she bravely hid a small pack of condoms beneath the bread rolls and silently prayed she could manage to pay for them without blushing. She was a twenty-seven-year-old woman having incredible, mind blowing sex, for crying out loud! She should be holding a parade in the main street.

Several picnic items later she met Adam at the checkout, a large handful of fresh fruit added to their basket as he charmed the middle aged woman behind the counter with a smile.

'Hi, there—' he glanced down and back up '—Mabel.'

Roane rolled her eyes, as much at who was ringing up their purchases as the beaming response he got. Well, if the world didn't know she was sleeping with Adam it was going to inside a matter of minutes. Mabel loved a good gossip. 'Mabel is a sensible married woman with four kids. That won't work on her.'

'Oh, I don't know, Roane.' Mable giggled like a school-girl. 'Nothing wrong with being friendly…'

Adam smirked smugly and Roane couldn't help but laugh. She'd been the one to tell him to try being friendly after all. It was just a rarity for him to do anything she suggested outside the bedroom.

He glanced down, cocked a brow at her and shook his head. 'I'll be right back.'

'Where'd you find *him*?' Mable asked in a whisper. 'He's gorgeous.'

And knew it too. But Roane couldn't help smiling again, the reason why suddenly hitting her. She was happy. With a pang of regret, she wondered how long it would last.

'We're friends.'

It wasn't a complete lie. They were getting on better than she would ever have imagined. Even more ridiculously she knew she would miss him when he was gone. Surely it was too fast to feel that way? Yeah, thought the girl who'd slept with him after three days. The usual rules didn't apply to someone like Adam and it seemed to have had a knock-on effect on Roane. She was behaving so completely out of character she felt a little lost for a moment.

Then Adam dumped a load of things into their basket and looked her straight in the eye.

Almost in slow motion Roane managed to forcibly drag her gaze away from the intense heat radiating off him. She looked down at the basket, stifling a groan and immediately feeling a wave of heat rise on her cheeks as she looked at Mabel's smiling face.

Who lifted the first bumper pack of many and rang it up on her till, without saying a single word. She didn't have to. The condoms said it all.

There was a loud crunch beside her and Roane glared at Adam as he chewed a mouthful of apple and spoke with his mouth full, waving the apple at Mabel as he stared at Roane. 'And this, Mabel.'

Roane continued to glare at him as he reached for his wallet. She was going to kill him.

Outside in the sunshine she lifted her chin high and informed him, '*You* are in *so* much trouble right now.'

He swallowed another mouthful of apple, studying his surroundings as they walked. 'You've never actually bought condoms, have you?'

'I've bought them *discreetly.*' She scowled at him, her cheeks still ridiculously hot. 'I haven't felt the need to announce to the entire island that I'm having—*sex!*'

When she looked around her and lowered her voice to hiss the word 'sex' at him he stopped and turned to consider her with hooded eyes. 'People have sex every day. If they're lucky they get to have it…'

He lifted a hand and made a show of counting his long fingers, the corners of his devilishly sexy mouth twitching as he gave up, dropped his hand and added, '*Lots.*'

When she couldn't stop looking at his mouth he tossed the half-eaten apple in a nearby receptacle and placed his hands on her hips, tugging her closer. 'In our case they only stop out of necessity. And, sweetheart? If I have my way—which you know I will—you'll be buying plenty more of that very necessity pretty damn soon. So you need to get used to it…'

Roane's jaw dropped. 'Are you kidding me? We just bought enough for a month.'

'No, we didn't. Couple of weeks' worth—tops.'

Ridiculously even the fact he was handing her a couple of weeks made her heart soar. 'Is that a fact?'

Adam nodded firmly. 'It is.'

Roane managed a shaky breath as he lowered his head and kissed her. Oh, Lord, she was in trouble. She couldn't possibly feel something so strong for him so fast. It wasn't how things were supposed to be.

His hand lifted, his knuckles brushing a strand of hair from her cheek when the wind caught it. Then he stepped closer, forcing her to tilt her head further back as he deepened the kiss and sought entry with the tip of his tongue. There it was: the instant spark—the spiralling knot of desire. The need to have his body joined to hers. If anything it was even stronger than it had been twenty-four hours ago, because now she knew what came next. She knew what it was like to have that warm mouth and his large hands on her body. How it felt when he pushed inside her. She could practically feel the weight of his body on hers as he drove her to the edge and beyond.

How was she supposed to survive without it now she knew what it felt like with him? How was she supposed to breathe without it hurting when he left? When every breath she currently took was filled with his enticing scent as he stole her heart piece by piece.

She knew nothing about him. *Nothing.*

She was falling for him. *Hard.*

When he lifted his head she forced a smile onto her face and gently extricated herself from his hold to step around him. 'Well, in that case...'

She bit her lip and smiled impishly over her shoulder. 'There was this ring thing in there that I think might have possibilities...according to the back of the pack it's for him *and* her...'

Deep laughter erupted from his chest as he reached for her

hand and yanked her back to him. 'We don't need it. Haven't you learned that yet?'

Laughing in reply, she stumbled as he slammed her body into his, his feet spreading wider to balance them both. 'And here I thought you liked it when I got adventurous. I don't remember you complaining when I—'

'Afternoon, Roane.'

Adam lifted his head as the owner of the voice passed them, Roane looking to see who it was. She scrunched her nose up and closed her eyes. 'Hi, Peter.'

When she opened her eyes Adam's were filled with silent sparkling laughter. 'Who was that?'

'My bank manager.'

'Ah.'

Ah indeed. But she didn't care, her chin jerking upwards as she huskily demanded, 'Kiss me.'

Another chuckle of deep laughter vibrated his chest and Roane smiled at him. She loved it when he laughed. But the firm kiss he gave her was all too brief and then he was slinging a long arm over her shoulders and tucking her into his side, lowering his head to her temple to promise her, *Later.* He steered them towards the motorcycle. 'Let's go build up an appetite first…and I don't mean for food…'

Roane leaned her head back against his shoulder, moving her arm around his lean waist and hooking her thumb under the belt loop of his jeans. 'We're having an early night, though, right?'

He chuckled again. 'I've created a monster.'

Roane was laughing with him when another voice sounded, 'A.J.? It is you. Thought so. What the hell you doing here, man?'

Adam changed in a heartbeat, releasing Roane and

frowning at her before he stepped forwards and shook the fair-haired man's hand. 'Just visiting. Didn't know you knew the island.'

'Wife's folks have a holiday place here. You should come out and see us. Lucy would be glad to see you.' He looked pointedly at Roane. 'Bring your girl over. Hi—Steve Rowland. I do business with A.J.'

Roane shook the hand that was offered to her. 'Roane Elliott.'

'Roane—lovely name.'

'Thank you.' She let go of his hand and stepped closer to Adam, looking up at his unreadable expression with a lift of her brow. 'How long have you known A.J.?'

'Too long.' He laughed as he looked at Adam. 'I meant to thank you for that last tip you gave me. You were right on the money—as always.'

'No problem.' Adam placed his palm on the small of Roane's back and exerted pressure to nudge her forwards. 'We've got to go. Tell Luce I said hi.'

'Stop by. We're in Oak Bluffs. You've got my cell.'

'Do. Bye, Steve.'

'Bye, Steve.' Roane leaned her head to one side to smile at him as she was firmly ushered away. 'Nice to meet you.'

'You too, Roane. Make him bring you along.'

'Oh, I will.' She looked up at Adam with open curiosity when they were a few steps away, 'A.J.?'

'It's how most people know me.'

'What's it stand for?'

He didn't look the least little bit pleased to be telling her, 'Adam Jameson.'

'Middle name?' She hadn't known that. The clench of his jaw made her smile. As middle names went she didn't think it was all that bad. But it obviously bothered Adam.

'And mother's maiden name.'

The words had been said on a flat tone that made Roane wonder what the problem was. Then it came to her. 'You don't use the Bryant name, do you?'

'No.'

They stopped beside the shining motorcycle, Roane frowning in confusion. 'Why?'

'Because it's easier.'

And because when he left the island he hadn't just left his home behind? He'd left everything. Had he really hated his father that much?

Roane's voice was low. 'I don't understand.'

'I wouldn't expect you to.' He shrugged, opening one of the storage cases at the back of his bike to stow away their purchases.

Reaching a hand to his outstretched arm, she gently squeezed to get his attention. 'Then make me. Did you really hate them that much?'

His gaze focused on her hand. 'Who?'

'Your dad—Jake—everyone who has the Bryant name. People would say the name opened doors for you...'

The words seemed to make him more tense than he already was, his spine straightening as he dropped his arm to his side and freed her hand. 'I'm not interested in opening those doors. Never was. I don't make my living piggybacking on a name. I do it my way.'

Instead of being intimidated by his change back to the surly man she'd met just days ago Roane stepped closer, her hands lifting to his waist and her voice still soft. 'Okay. So what *do you* do?'

He smiled, but his eyes were serious. When he spoke his voice shimmered with authority, hinting that whatever it was he did he did from a high position. 'I dabble in whatever interests me. And I do it well.'

Meaning he didn't want her to know.

The sense of rejection must have shown in her eyes, because his hands immediately lifted to frame her face, his thumbs tilting her chin up as he leaned down to look into her eyes. 'It's complicated.'

Roane frowned. 'You don't think I'm clever enough to understand, do you? I might not have a genius IQ like you do, Adam, but that doesn't mean—'

He kissed her to shut her up. 'I know it doesn't. That's not what I meant.'

'So what, then—you're a spy?'

The corners of his mouth twitched. 'Not a spy. It's much less interesting than that.'

'Then wh—?'

Another kiss. Much as Roane enjoyed the liberties he was taking to distract her from the subject, she was starting to get annoyed. What was the big deal? Was he really so determined not to let her into a single corner of his life? It wasn't as if she was going to stalk him all over the country after he left!

'I'll tell you. Just not now.' He took a deep breath that brushed his chest against her breasts. 'Do us both a favour and don't push.'

Who *was* this man? It hit her that she was sleeping with a stranger. Surely that should have scared her more than it did?

'It's nothing illegal.'

'Nothing illegal.' He looked amused at the idea.

'Or unethical…'

'Nope; not my style.'

'Or immoral.'

Adam shook his head, a lopsided smile appearing to addle her thoughts. 'Good to know you have such a high opinion of me. No—nothing immoral—and you're pushing, sweetheart.'

When he reached for her helmet and set it against her breasts she cocked her head and smiled at him to cover up how confused she suddenly felt. A day with Adam was quite the magical mystery tour, wasn't it? She just wished it didn't leave her feeling as if he didn't trust her. 'So are we visiting Steve and Lucy?'

'No.' Adam continued smiling as he reached for his helmet. 'Feed him a couple of beers and you'll get information about my life I *definitely* don't want you knowing.'

'Like stories about women.'

'Among others…'

Great, and now she was jealous of unseen women who had absolutely nothing to do with her. But they knew him in his new life—which meant they knew him better than she did. Roane hated them for that.

A thought made her shudder. 'Have you ever been married?'

'Hell, no.' He frowned at her. 'Where did that come from?'

Roane ignored the frown. 'Kids? Don't say not that you know of…'

'If there was even the remotest chance of me having a child I'd know about it—' the frown darkened '—and I'd be there. Want to tell me where you're going with this?'

'Am I allowed to know anything about you or are secrets part of the deal?'

'What damn deal?'

She knew she was starting an argument but she couldn't seem to stop herself from doing it, an emotional cocktail of frustration, confusion and hurt mixing together and forming anger. 'The "you teach, I learn" deal—the one where you get to fill in a few hours before you leave again.'

The control he exerted over his anger was admirable, but the muscle clenching on his jaw told her just how much it was costing him. 'You knew I'd leave when we started this.'

He was right. She did. By saying what she had she'd just told him how involved she was, hadn't she?

With great effort and the performance of a lifetime she buried how she felt. 'I did. You're right.'

After a long moment of tense silence, Adam shook his head, his profile turned to her as he fought some kind of inner battle before looking her in the eye again. Then the soft rumble of sincerity entered his voice.

'I can't give you more than this. It's not that I don't want to. I can't.'

Roane blinked at him. She knew he meant what he said, she could hear it in his voice, see it in the intensity of his gaze. Ridiculously she felt as if she would know if Adam was lying to her. How could she know that?

But what really got to her was she could feel such a strong sense of *emptiness* in him. It was the most dreadful sensation. She immediately felt the need to make him feel better, to wrap herself around him and stay there until she couldn't feel it in him any more.

Pursing his lips into a thin line, he looked away and then back; even the minutest hint of uncertainty in a man so sure of himself was heartbreaking to behold.

'I can give you now.'

She didn't hesitate. 'I'll take it.'

His eyes softened to a darker brown than she'd ever seen before, then he nodded. 'Good.'

Roane knew she'd take whatever she could get, she was already that addicted to him. She just had to remember not to allow herself to think about the fact that every day had a 'now'.

A genius like Adam should have known that too, shouldn't he?

CHAPTER TEN

IT FELT AS IF Roane was changing something in him.

Adam had no idea why he'd said the things he had in the Haven. Or why it was he'd felt as if he had to tell her the things he knew he couldn't. For a brief moment he'd wanted to tell her *everything*—every last detail. He'd never done that—*with anyone.*

It had been a roller coaster of a day. He'd made love to her in the open air as the sun came up, had let her make love to him and been astonished by just how quick a study she really was.

Then he'd spent the time on his motorcycle excruciatingly aroused by her pressed so tightly to his back. He'd even contemplated keeping driving until they were far away and no one could find them until he'd sated them both.

More surprising than anything else, he'd had fun with her on their shopping expedition, had felt—happy was the right word, he supposed. Yes, that was it. He'd been happy spending time with her doing something completely mundane, brief as it was. He couldn't remember the last time he'd felt that way—if he ever had.

Then they'd met Steve. He couldn't risk meeting someone

from the city when it was so important Adam hold onto his anonymity. Of course Roane was curious. How could she not be? Especially when Adam couldn't tell her about his job—not that he wasn't prepared to; he wanted her to know about the life he'd made for himself. He was proud of that life, of the things he'd achieved. He'd worked hard. But she was too tied to his family—he wouldn't let her get caught in the middle of the battle looming on the horizon.

As it was she didn't think he trusted her, did she? When it had nothing to do with trust—he trusted her. A somewhat miraculous change of personality for someone who trusted as little as Adam did. By holding back from her he'd hurt her—and he'd hated that.

He'd found himself holding his breath while he waited for her to choose what they already had, because he wanted it. He wanted it more than he'd wanted anything in a very long time.

Familiar frustration had bubbled inside him like boiling acid for a long while afterwards, even when she'd made her decision so fast. Until the soothing balm that was Roane worked its magic on him and he let himself get lost in a surreal world where for a brief moment he actually felt—content. She was amazing. All the more so because she had no idea of the miraculous effect she had on him.

He'd never been content a day in his life.

By the time they got back to the estate he was burning up with the need to demonstrate how she'd made him feel. He wanted to make her feel as good as she'd made him feel. In the absence of words or emotion it was the only gift he could give her.

But Jake was waiting in the guest house. And Adam barely had time to release the small hand he was holding before a fist made contact with his jaw.

'*Jake!*' Roane yelled and stepped forwards. 'What are you *doing*?'

Adam lifted an arm and hauled her back to his side, almost as if he was stating where she belonged. 'Don't.'

He then glared at his little brother. 'First one's free. Next one will cost you.'

Roane tried to pull free, her eyes wide as she looked from Adam's jaw to Jake's face. 'What the hell was that for?'

'Ask *him*.' Jake's face was dark with anger. 'Go on. Ask him what he's been doing.'

Her wide-eyed gaze swung to Adam, a million and one questions silently being asked in the blue depths. 'What's he talking about?'

Adam knew. Someone *had* been doing some digging, hadn't they? But he wasn't going to let her get caught in the middle, it was the very reason he hadn't told her himself. 'Leave. *Now.*'

'*No.*' She lifted her chin and defied his firm tone.

'I mean it. Go.'

'No. She stays. She's part of it, after all, isn't she, big brother?'

Adam felt a wave of anger crashing in on him. 'She has *nothing* to do with it.'

'No?' Jake's tone was laced with sarcasm. 'I saw you two in Tisbury. Seducing her is another way of getting at me, isn't it?'

Adam didn't much care for the insinuation, stepping forwards and pushing Roane behind him. He then fought to keep his voice cool and his words as clear as possible. 'I didn't do anything to get at you. That wasn't what I was doing.'

'Then what *were* you doing?' Jake stood his ground, his hands bunched in readiness at his sides.

Roane got loose, and before Adam could do anything to stop it she was standing between them. In the face of bristling anger radiating from the two large males she bravely lifted her chin and glared in warning at each of them in turn. 'Okay. Which one of you wants to tell me what's going on? Because I swear—I'm ready to cause actual bodily harm if one of you doesn't start acting like an adult.'

They both looked down at her, Roane not the least bit fazed by the fact she had to lift her chin higher to continue glaring at them. Under normal circumstances Adam would have smiled, hauled her close and kissed her hard for how beautiful she looked with that much fire in her eyes. She was feisty, his girl.

Instead he frowned at her. 'Leave, Roane. It's the last time I'm gonna say it.'

But again she defied him. 'And let you both pummel each other into a pulp? I think not. You're *brothers*! Tell me what's going on.'

Adam swore under his breath and looked at Jake, repeating his words through clenched teeth. 'I didn't do it to get at you.'

Jake had the guts to laugh sarcastically, which Adam begrudgingly respected him for. They weren't so different, were they? He'd been known to laugh in someone's face mid-argument. In fact, if there was a way to escalate things through sarcasm Adam was pretty much the master.

'Okay, then.' Jake nodded, his eyes narrow and his jaw tight. 'Let's just work our way through the facts, shall we? You knew I was head of the company.'

'Yes.'

'Then tell me how it wasn't to get to me?'

'I'm telling you it wasn't.'

'So what was it, then? To prove you're the better man? Revenge? To step in and take over? If you wanted the job so bad, then all you had to do was stay—it was yours. It was yours by birth, for crying out loud!'

That was an archaic notion, Adam thought. The way he saw it, their father was happier with Jake at the helm, Jake was happy being there, Adam was free to do as he chose. The world was the way it was meant to be.

Roane's voice rose. 'Would *someone* please tell me what's going on?'

When Adam remained impassive Jake jerked his brows in challenge and then looked at her. 'Okay, then. I'll tell you. The company has been fighting off takeover rumours since Dad got sick. Share prices dropped when I took over—I had to prove myself. Then there were whispers someone had been buying, they'd been buying for years. Small numbers, but collectively they added up to a threat. That's why I needed *him*...' he jerked his chin at Adam '...back here to talk about selling his shares to me. Dad signed half the family shares to each of us when he wrapped up his affairs.'

Adam was still staring Jake down when he caught sight of Roane's head turning. He could feel her gaze burning into him but he didn't look at her. He couldn't take the chance—because if there was so much as a flicker of doubt in her eyes he would feel the need to hit something...

He clenched his teeth when realization laced her words with disbelief. 'You were buying the shares?'

Jake cocked his head to the side and studied Adam with malice. 'And along with his family shares he now owns the majority. You're looking at the Bryant who holds the reins. Question is: is he planning on riding the horse—or shooting it?'

Instead of any of the questions Adam had been expecting from Roane she asked, 'How did you afford—?'

Jake smiled at her, but it was anything but warm. Adam silently dared him to say a single thing that would cause her pain. *Go on. Give me a reason not to stand here and let you get it all out in one go…*

'Didn't he mention that part? Turns out my big brother is a bona-fide multibillionaire. He could buy the Bryant Corporation with what would be the equivalent of chump change to him. Right, Adam?'

The room fell into the kind of silence that sat oppressively in the air, Roane's small voice eventually sounding beside him, 'Adam?'

'He prefers A.J. these days. Hates us that much he won't even use the family name, will you—' Jake stepped forwards and practically spat the word in his face '—*Jameson*? What I'd like to know is what we did to you. Leaving wasn't enough? You had to work from the outside to bring us down and then come back to use someone who's more a part of this family than you ever were and hurt her too? What did she ever do to you? Why couldn't you *leave her be*?'

Because it felt *right,* goddammit! For the first time in his life he'd come home and felt as if he *belonged.*

As if he'd come back *to her*!

The truth of it hit him like a blow to the chest. Adam had had enough. He lifted his hands and pushed Jake back a step— not with any degree of force, but with enough controlled strength to move him out of Adam's face. 'You leave her out of this!'

It happened in the blink of an eye. When Jake lifted his arm to swing, Roane reached out. Before Adam could move she was on her rear on the floor, a squeak of surprised outrage leaving her lips. He hadn't hit her, but when he'd swung his arm back from her hold Jake had inadvertently knocked her over.

Adam saw red.

'Son-of-a—' He knelt down and reached for her, frustration rising to boiling point when she shrugged away from his touch.

'Don't touch me, Adam.'

'Are you—?'

'I'm *fine!*'

It only marginally appeased him when she did the same thing with Jake when he reached for her. 'Don't *you* touch me either!'

She struggled ungracefully to her feet and absent-mindedly rubbed her behind as she blew a strand of hair out of her eyes and glared at them both. 'I hope you feel awful for knocking me on my ass, Jacob Bryant. You're both *pathetic!*' She folded her arms, her cheeks flushed as she fixed Adam with a furious gaze. 'Is it true? You're some kind of squillionaire?'

Adam fought for some semblance of control. 'Yes.'

'Since when?'

'I inherited some money when I turned twenty-one—from my mother's estate.' Hadn't been much after her lavish lifestyle, but it had given him a start. 'I dabbled in the markets and commodities—invested—I'm good at what I do. There are patterns I can understand.'

Jake began to pace.

But Roane kept looking at Adam as if she was barely aware there was anyone else there. 'And the shares you bought in the Bryant Corporation?'

'I'd heard rumours the old man's touch was slipping, so I bought where I could. When Jake took over the word on the street was someone would try a takeover. So I bought enough to make sure it wouldn't happen unless it was me.'

Her eyes narrowed. 'Why?'

Adam glanced at Jake and saw he'd stopped pacing, his hooded eyes studying Adam with caution. He wasn't prepared to explain himself to his younger brother. Let Jake think what he wanted.

'Well?'

He didn't look at her. 'We're done here.'

There was no way to avoid walking past his brother to get to the stairs so Adam straightened his spine, staring straight at him and daring him to make a move.

But Roane wasn't done. 'Go away, Jake.'

'I'm not—'

'Yes, you are. I'll feel safer if I only have one of you to deal with at a time. But don't think I'm done with you—'cause I'm not.' She took a breath. 'Adam and I need to talk and he won't while you're here.'

Under normal circumstances Adam wouldn't have talked to her either after that kind of insight. But she deserved better. So he didn't say anything as he kept walking, ignoring Jake when he dropped in a low warning, 'Hurt her and I'll hunt you down—got it?'

Said the guy who'd knocked her over? Now there was irony. But Adam shook his head and kept walking. The kid had never known when he was out of his league; he had ended up with dozens of black eyes and bloody noses that had never taught him a lesson in school or at camp. Gutsy but stupid—that was Jake as a kid, and there'd been a time when Adam had found it amusing in an almost affectionate, brotherly kind of way.

But those days were gone.

Now he would for evermore associate Jake with the rage

he'd felt at seeing Roane on the floor. If she'd been hurt in any way—well, Adam didn't like to think what he'd have done. Accidental or not—Jake had done it. But then Adam would never forgive himself for inadvertently putting her in the middle. He'd *tried* not to. He'd *tried* to protect her. He'd failed.

Now he was going to have to tell her the answers to everything she asked as penance instead of because he wanted to. Then they'd be done. No more 'now'. He'd leave and she'd stay and 'they' would be something amazing that happened in a few days on Martha's Vineyard—in his memories, in the past…

Adam had no idea why knowing that felt so bad.

Roane waited for Jake to leave, her foot tapping on the floor while she was torn in different directions. She knew Jake hadn't pushed her over on purpose but she hated the momentary fear she'd felt. Jake had some major grovelling to do and he knew it.

He was the easy one.

Her gaze rose to the top of the stairs. What to do about Adam—that was the more difficult question. Walking away would definitely be the easier option, but she couldn't. She didn't want to believe he was the kind of man Jake thought he was. Not the Adam who'd made love to her with so much tenderness. He couldn't be that vengeful. It couldn't be true. If it was her faith in mankind was about to be shattered.

She was already caught between the devil and the deep blue sea. Jake was like a brother to her—had been her best friend for years. Adam was her lover—in the truest sense of the word she'd ever experienced or probably ever would again. She didn't want them at each other's throats.

To her surprise he wasn't packing. Instead he was in the library-cum-office, standing behind a desk staring out a window. His stance was rigid, defensive; sunlight streaming through the windows to illuminate his profile and highlight the blond in his hair. Yes, still beautiful to her, but the loneliness in him was heartbreaking. Was that what she'd felt earlier?

He didn't turn, but he knew she was there, the flat tone of his deep voice striking at a chord inside her. 'You shouldn't have got caught in that.'

'But I did.'

'Ask whatever you want. I'll answer. It's up to you if you choose to believe it.'

Now he was an open book? It was too much of a temptation to resist. The burning need to know everything drew her further into the room.

'Well, we've covered how you make your living, not that you need to do anything…'

'Everyone needs to do something.'

'You left the second you inherited, didn't you?'

'I wasn't that patient; I left before the paperwork was through. I took work where I could find it and thought about what I wanted to do and the kind of man I wanted to be.'

She watched as he lifted his arms and pushed his hands into his pockets. 'I never lived up to the Bryant name here so it made sense not to carry it out there. The old man helped with that decision.'

'How?'

He shrugged, 'He spent a lot of time telling me what a disappointment I was—not that he wasn't pushed. I had attitude back then. Still do some would say…'

Roane's steps faltered when she was able to see his face.

He was so calm. So detached. As if he were talking about someone else's life and none of it mattered. How could he be so cold? It suddenly hit her: *control.* He'd taught himself to exert so much control he was able to appear unfeeling on the surface. Everything he thought and felt was hidden away.

It made her long to know what lay underneath.

She silently cleared her throat and braved another step closer. 'I'm sure he didn't mean it.'

'People have a tendency to state the harsher truths in the heat of the moment.'

'You have to know he's regretted it ever since. He told you he felt he'd let you down.'

'"Every man is guilty of all the good he didn't do."' He glanced sideways at her, warily or with resignation? Roane couldn't decide which one it was as he added, 'Voltaire again.'

When he looked back out the window she stilled, waiting. Eventually he glanced sideways at her again. But he didn't say anything. Meaning he wouldn't volunteer the information unless she asked the questions. Okay. She'd known this wasn't going to be easy.

'So you took your inheritance and invested it and made buckets of money. You have a base of operations?' She remembered something he'd said. 'Do you have offices in New York?'

He looked back out the window. 'I don't have an office. The people who work for me have them. I have places I stay. An apartment in New York overlooking Central Park, another in San Francisco—a house in New Orleans; cities I like—I told you that.'

Not all of it, he hadn't. Therein lay the rub as far as Roane was concerned. Why couldn't he have told her these things? Why did he have to make it so darn difficult? He'd given her small pieces of the puzzle, had never lied, but had never told the truth either. Was he like that with everyone or just the ones he was determined not to get emotionally involved with?

'The project you told me about in New Orleans—the one where you made those friends you swapped bracelets with—was that rebuilding your house after Katrina?'

'No. I donated twenty million dollars to a fund for the rebuilding of schools and low-rent communities. I work the sites when I get a chance. The friends were from the communities we helped.'

Twenty million dollars, he made it sound as if it were nothing. Yet he didn't flaunt his money, didn't run around with a chauffeur-driven limo—he could have been any guy on the street. Okay, maybe not *any guy*...but he wasn't like any billionaire Roane had ever met. The Vineyard had its share of them...

Adam took a breath and turned, sitting down on the edge of the window seat and lifting his chin to study her with hooded eyes. 'Next question.'

Roane's breath hitched. 'Don't you dare take that attitude with me.'

'What attitude? You sent Jake scurrying off so you could ask questions, so ask them.' Infuriatingly he smiled the lazy smile that had always sent her pulse skipping. 'You wanted to know plenty this afternoon—now's your big chance. The secret's out now.'

A realization hit her so hard she almost rocked back on her feet with the force of it. 'You didn't trust me not to tell Jake. You thought I'd pick a side. That's why you wouldn't tell me anything this afternoon.'

'If that's your opinion of me again—' his eyes narrowed dangerously '—I think we're done here. I'm obviously exactly the kind of guy who would spend years plotting his revenge on his family and who'd bring down his brother just to prove he's the better man. I should really have dressed in black from head to toe for the full effect, shouldn't I?'

Pushing to his feet, he removed his hands from his pockets and stepped around the huge oak desk. 'Of course seducing you was obviously part of my great plan to wreak havoc too—just like Jake said. I'm one helluva guy, aren't I?'

But the man he'd described wasn't the man who'd made love to her. She knew him. As if by stripping away layers of clothing he'd bared more than his glorious body to her. A man that driven on destruction could never have touched her heart the way he had. If he thought he was scaring her away, then he could just think again.

She folded her arms and took a deep breath as he reached the door. 'Are you done?'

For a second she thought he would keep walking—it was what he'd done for most of his life, after all—but after a moment he turned, leaning his shoulder nonchalantly against the door jamb. 'More, is there?'

'Tell me why you did it.'

'Plotted against my family, planned Jake's demise or seduced you? I might need you to narrow it down for me.'

Instinctively Roane knew the only way she was going to snap him out of the control he was exerting was to goad him into anger. It was a risky move; she'd seen him downstairs and he had one heck of a temper. When he'd seen her on the floor—

He'd been mad as hell she was on the floor. He had been concerned she might be hurt, yes, but it was more than that. She felt a smile blossoming inside her as a flicker of hope sparked to life. But smiling wouldn't help her cause so she damped it down and lifted her chin, 'Throw many of these pity parties, do we?'

There was a flash of green in his eyes. It was all the proof she needed that she was on the right track. His eyes would change colour: emerald-green flashing in the brown when he was angry, brown softening the green to a mossy tone when he was turned on, brown clouding the green out altogether when he was laughing...Roane knew so many of the meanings, *already*.

Right now she was rattling the tiger's cage.

'Get to the point, sweetheart. I have a bag to pack.'

She nodded. 'Yes, 'cause that's what you do best, isn't it? You run away.'

Large hands curled into fists at his sides, fingers uncurling and stretching when he saw she'd noticed. He wasn't even prepared to show that much of a loss of his precious control, was he?

'When did goading me seem like a good idea to you?'

Roane searched the air above his head, moving her head from shoulder to shoulder while she considered her answer. 'Oh, I dunno. Maybe round about the time you started acting like an ass again. In the absence of a rudder to kick a girl has to get creative.'

There was a brief narrowing of his eyes and then he lowered his chin and stalked towards her. It wasn't all that long ago it would have jumped her heart into her throat, but she stood her ground and willed her thundering heart to stay where it was.

'Intimidating me won't work this time either. I'm a new woman. You helped with that some, but being knocked on your ass will do it too, I've discovered. Always wondered where the phrase "knock some sense into you" came from...'

He clenched his jaw, hard, stopping a couple of feet away from her. 'Maybe you should just tell me what it is you want from me.'

'I want you to stop holding back from me. Last night I thought we'd agreed we wouldn't do that.'

'In *bed*. This isn't the same thing.'

'That's a cop-out and you know it is.' She felt anger billowing up inside her, frustration carrying her feet forwards. 'Tell me why you did it, Adam—the real reason. Look me in the eye and I'll know you're telling me the truth.'

The cruel smile bared his teeth. 'You think I can't look you in the eye and lie? *Still* have a lot to learn, don't you, little girl?'

'You won't.' She stopped a foot away, shaking inside as she forced back the tears of frustration threatening behind her eyes. If she got this wrong and pushed him further away from her it was going to hurt. She just needed to find a way to reach him. 'I know you won't.'

'How can you?' The full force of his anger roared the words into the still room, his eyes flashing sparks of green fire and the cords of his neck strained. 'You've known me *four days*!'

Roane faced the storm by summoning every ounce of strength she had in her. 'You think this makes any sense to me? It doesn't. I know it's too fast and too soon and at least a dozen other things that don't make any more sense than the last. But I just know—*I feel it!* There's no way to explain that—it's just there. If I didn't trust you I would never have slept with you!'

When a tear slipped off the edge of her lashes she swiped angrily at it. 'Even when I didn't like you I trusted you with my body. Because it *felt right*. I wasn't wrong about that, Adam—I *know* I wasn't...'

Even as her voice lowered to a harsh whisper at the end, the memory of their lovemaking sent a rush of heat tingling over her skin. Whatever else he was, Adam was an incredible lover; he'd touched her as though she were infinitely fragile, kissed her until she could hardly breathe... He'd stolen a part of her in one night. So, yes, she'd been absolutely right to trust her body to him. There wasn't a single doubt in her mind.

He looked as if he was ready to hit something, but Roane kept going, her voice stronger but cracking on some of the words. 'I wasn't wrong to trust you with my body. I'm not wrong about this. So look me in the eye and tell me why you did it and I'll believe you—even if it's something I end up hating you for.'

When he turned his face towards the open window she could feel the deep-seated need for flight in him. Just by looking where he was looking he was telling her—even if it was subconsciously—he was ready to leave. And how much more of an effort it would take to stay.

She silently begged him to make that effort. Because he didn't have to be alone—he had her—didn't he know that? He'd had her from the get-go.

A muscle jumped in his jaw, his impossibly thick lashes flickered as his gaze moved to random points in the room, he pursed his lips into a thin line and then finally—*finally*—he looked her straight in the eye and the deep rumble of his voice spoke the words she'd hoped to hear.

'I did it to keep it safe.'

Her lower lip trembled. 'To protect the company.'

'Yes.'

'Because you could.' She nodded. 'Not because you wanted it for yourself or because you didn't want Jake to have it.'

'Yes.'

The inner shaking had worked its way into her chest so that breathing became difficult. 'You were looking out for the family, weren't you? No matter what you say or do, it still matters to you…'

He looked back out the window.

Roane cleared her throat and blinked to clear her vision. 'If it mattered so much why didn't you come home? You were gone for twelve years.'

When he looked at her the truth sent a chill over her entire body, goose-bumps breaking out on her arms. 'Oh, my God. You did come home, didn't you?' She breathed the question, 'When?'

'I've been on the island at least once a year.' He shrugged. 'I've always liked the Vineyard…'

She stepped closer and could have wept when he stepped out of her reach. 'Why didn't you come *home*? They would never have turned you away. I think your father secretly tried to find you—maybe he did and couldn't face you, I don't know for sure. And Jake—'

Her voice broke. 'Why do you think he was so angry downstairs? He was hurting. He hero-worshipped you when he was a kid—you should have heard the way he talked about you. When you left—it felt like you'd left *him*. He didn't understand why. For a while I think he thought *he'd* done something wrong. That if he'd done something different he could have stopped you…'

Adam frowned at her, his voice rough. 'He didn't do anything wrong. I didn't leave him. I left the ring.'

'What ring?' She shook her head, her gaze dropping to the ring Adam was twisting almost absent-mindedly with a thumb curled into his palm. Her brows wavered. 'That's what the ring is? It's for Jake?'

She'd known that everything he wore had meaning. Friendship, family legacies—the things he valued…

'It's a Celtic symbol for brotherhood. I left him one in that dumb-ass tree house he got me to help build. Who the hell has a tree house at fourteen anyway?' He shook his head. '*Loser.* It was in an envelope with instructions how to find me if he ever needed me.'

Roane remembered the second he said it. She remembered the names they would toss at each other. *Jerk,* Jake would call Adam. *Loser,* Adam would reply. She'd forgotten that. At thirteen she'd thought they were both dorks. They'd spent weeks and weeks building that dumb tree house two years before Adam left. Jake had taken a crowbar to it a month after he'd finally accepted he wasn't coming back. He'd never found the message his brother had left him. He'd have told her if he had.

He'd have been so happy.

A choking sob broke free from her chest when she understood the gravity of the one clue that had been missed. Things could have been so different. 'But when he didn't come find you, you thought…'

She couldn't even finish the sentence.

Adam's brows jerked as realization set in. 'Right.'

That was all he had to say? *Right?* Then his mouth twitched as if he was about to smile. Surely he wasn't seeing it as ironic? She would have to slap him if he did. It wasn't ironic—it was incredibly sad—for both of the brothers she loved.

Before the impact of that hit her she got another word from Adam: 'Okay.'

'Right and okay? Are you *kidding me?*'

'What do you want me to say?' He frowned at her. 'I can't change history. It's just a variable I hadn't considered, that's all.'

A variable he hadn't considered? Blinking in astonishment, Roane shook her head to clear her thoughts.

'But you can build some bridges now. Tell him. I'm not saying he'll make it easy for you—you have a lot in common that way—but tell him. Stay and try.'

The words faded into the silence and Roane watched as he worked the suggestion through his mind a few times. Half his problem was that incredibly large brain of his, she decided. He over-thought things. But just when she was about to say that he looked at her with the intense heat that curled her toes—

She knew his thoughts had turned to her.

A distinct sense of impending doom hit Roane, her heart twisting painfully in anticipation of being told she'd gone too far—it was none of her business—he was leaving anyway…

They were done.

CHAPTER ELEVEN

ADAM MOVED TO the edge of the desk and sat down, his legs wide and his forearms on his thighs so that his large hands dangled between his knees. Then he considered her, slowly, silently, until Roane thought she might scream if he didn't say something…

'Even if I try some bridge-building, I'll still leave. You need to understand that.'

Trying to hide the fact the words hurt like hell, Roane nodded. 'I know. You have a life.'

'I do.'

'And responsibilities.' Like the work he did in New Orleans. Roane wondered if he had any idea how impressed she was by that. Or how proud. He really was the most incredible man she'd ever met.

'Yes.'

'I know.' She said the words softly and smiled at him, almost afraid to break contact with his amazing eyes. She loved his eyes.

They narrowed a barely perceptible amount and then his silent study continued where it had left off. Only this time he took a deep breath and lifted a hand to rub his palm over his face, suddenly looking incredibly weary to her. It made her fingers itch to reach for him, to touch and to soothe and, well…

Touching him had only ever led to the one place.

Except now there was an even greater distance between them than before—and for all her bravado and determination when it came to Adam and his family, when it came to her tentative relationship with him…

Roane was scared silly.

Then he was on his feet, pacing the room like a caged animal with frustration radiating off his large body in waves. He frowned as he looked at her. 'I told you I can't give you more than this.'

'I know you did.'

'Staying wouldn't change that. I can't give you what I don't have to give.'

Roane didn't understand what he was saying. But judging by the way he was pacing, frowning, and searching the air with a completely focused gaze, he was working his way up to something. So she willed herself to stay absolutely still and wait, while her palms went clammy and her heart beat erratically.

'You'd want more. This wasn't supposed to be anything more.'

'I know.' She did. But he was right; she would want more. She was slowly dying without it already.

Adam was flexing his long fingers in and out of fists. 'See, that's what I don't get. Why are you trying to build bridges between me and my family when you know that'll bring me back here more often? You know what'll happen if I do. You're not that dumb.'

Roane had to clear her throat when he turned and looked at her, anger and confusion clouding his eyes. 'What will happen?'

'This will happen.' His deep voice was threaded with frustration. 'Every time. Because I've only to look at you and I want you. You can't tell me some part-time affair is what you want.'

'It's not.' She wouldn't lie to him. Even if she could she wouldn't after his confession of how much he wanted her physically.

'The thing is, you can tell me to leave you be, but even if I say I will I won't stick to it; you fight me off—I'll probably want you more. I know me.'

'I'm not fighting, in case you hadn't noticed.'

'Why *aren't* you?' He leaned forwards to shout the words at her and the force of his frustration was a shocking thing to behold. Not that she thought he would do her any harm, she knew he wouldn't. It was the ferocity of his emotion, the echoing emptiness, the need in him—all mixed into one and let loose as if they'd been held inside for decades that did it.

That was what made her step closer.

To where he stood his ground and kept going. 'What you want from me *I can't give you.* I've told you that. Yet here you are—you chose to side with someone you barely know over someone you've been friends with your whole life.'

'It wasn't about picking a side.' She stopped in front of him and tilted her head back. 'It was about being where I wanted to be most. Where I knew I was needed most. You needed me to believe in you, didn't you?'

He frowned dangerously at her, pulse pounding at the base of his neck, muscle jumping in his square jaw, hooded gaze fixed on hers.

Despite the fact Roane could feel the raging storm being held inside him again, she set her palm on his chest above his thundering heart and told him in a low, firm voice, 'I believe in what's in here.'

The kiss wasn't gentle. He kissed her with desperation, hard and fast—demanding her response. Heat immediately shot through her with stunning speed, every thought blown clear out of her mind.

Adam groaned and walked her back until she was trapped between him and the wall; his hands in her hair, her arms tight around his neck as she gave in to the need to give as much as she was receiving. Then one of his hands left her hair, sliding down to cup her breast. No foreplay, no teasing—and Roane's heart soared when she realized he wasn't holding back. It was all of his pent up emotions thrown into one kiss, he was raw and wild and uncontrolled—that was how much he needed her. No man had ever needed her that badly. It equalled how inconceivably much she needed him after so little time, as if she couldn't breathe without him there.

It gave her the courage to show him.

So she moved her hands under his arms, the already tense muscles of his back clenching beneath her fingers as she traced the width of his shoulders. But it wasn't enough. Moaning in frustration she tried to free his shirt from his arms, but even when he moved to help her and it was tossed to one side, it still wasn't enough.

The heat of the smooth male skin on his arms beneath her hands enflamed her—but it still wasn't enough. So she dropped her palms to his stomach and pushed him to make room as she reached for the bottom of his T-shirt.

Adam broke his lips free from hers and grasped the hem of her sweater. 'Off.'

'You too.' She let go of him long enough to tug her sweater over her head, reappearing to discover he'd done as he was told. But it was the look on his face that undid her; the rumble of his voice a low, sexual growl that sent shivers down her spine.

'You're so beautiful.'

He stared at her body with something close to reverence. Seeing how the sight of her affected him Roane had never felt so beautiful. She loved how she looked through his eyes. Any whisper of inhibition she had left fled before the sight of his naked desire. She had to see him, touch him; have him deep inside her.

'You have no idea how much I want you right now.' She let her gaze slide lovingly over the ripples of hard muscle beneath golden skin.

'Show me.'

Leaning forward she kissed her favourite place on his neck, impulsively running her tongue up the strong column of his throat. He groaned something she couldn't hear and then lifted her off her feet and held her high against the wall with one arm around her waist. Her breasts on a level with his mouth, Roane gripped his shoulders as he leaned in and suckled her through her bra, the abrasion of wet lace against her already hard nipple making her gasp out loud and writhe against him.

'Adam!'

Her already dizzy mind whirled as he spun round. Marching determinedly across the room, he lowered her to the desk. Roane didn't resist when he leaned forwards and pressed her down, didn't release her grip on his shoulders; she didn't do anything beyond murmuring words of encouragement before touching him everywhere she could reach.

His hands slid over her ribs and across her belly as he switched his attention to her other breast. So swept away was she by the glorious sense of abandon she felt that it was only when he unfastened her jeans and started to tug them away that she realized she'd lifted her legs and wrapped them around his hips. But then everything with Adam had always seemed so natural to her. Sexually there were surely no two people better matched on the face of the earth than they were.

Somehow he managed to reposition her, dragging denim and lace off as one. Better, but still not enough. She was on fire, so much so that she almost sobbed with impatience during the seconds it took for him to leave her and shed his own jeans. Filled with a violent, possessive drive she'd never felt before, she hauled him back down to her and kissed him hard. Feverish and insane with need, she wanted to bite, scratch, brand him with a visible mark if she had to so that the whole world knew he was *hers*—even if he wasn't. But for *now* he was. She would never forget him as long as she lived.

Adam didn't try to calm her down or slow the frantic pace of what was happening—if anything he seemed to welcome it. Apparently he considered it either too much trouble or too time-consuming to reach round and unhook her bra, so instead he tugged the straps down, freeing her breasts for his hungry mouth.

To Roane's ears the sounds she made as his lips and his tongue worked their magic barely sounded human, let alone as if they were coming from her; it *still wasn't enough*. Would she ever get enough of him? When she reached for him he caught her wrists and pinned them above her head with a growl of warning that reverberated through her body everywhere his touched. Roane then shocked even herself by retaliating with a nip of his shoulder, a sharp intake of breath turning into a deep groan of approval as he covered her body with the full weight of his.

When she lifted her hips and dug her heels into the small of his back he groaned again. When he rocked his pelvis against hers, his hard length sliding only inches from where she wanted it, she moaned into his ear and arched her spine off the desk.

'Please.' Obeying a deep instinct that told her just how to entice him most, she rocked her hips up in invitation, coating his length in her slick heat. 'Please, Adam. I need you.'

Adam lifted his head and looked down at her, flexing his fingers around hers where their joined hands lay on the desk over her head. He looked so deep into her eyes she felt as if he could see her soul, but Roane didn't try to hide from him. While joint ragged breathing filled the silence she looked back at him, her smile trembling on her lips as she silently told him:

I love you.

Adam's brows wavered. Then he dropped his head and devoured her mouth, made a guttural sound in the base of his throat, and rested his forehead on hers as the confession was wrenched from deep inside him. 'I need you too.'

With one sudden thrust he sank deep into her, releasing her hands to tangle one hand in her hair and wrap an arm tight around her waist. The sudden fullness, the hard rhythm he set, how tight he held her—it was so overwhelming that he had her whimpering against his mouth as he tangled his tongue with hers.

It was fast and furious and primal and within moments she was wrenching her mouth from his to throw her head back and cry out with the force of her release. Again and again the waves came, making her writhe like a wild thing against him. She dug her nails into his back as he continued to thrust into her, hard and fast. He nipped, then suckled the hollow between her throat and her shoulder so hard she was sure he would leave the very brand she'd wanted to put on him, but she didn't care. Because the fire still pounded through her veins, her writhing was matching his thrusts, she was pushing against the desk to get her hips higher so he could go deeper. When she honestly thought she might pass out from an excess of pleasure, Adam lifted his head, groaned loudly into her hair and his body went rigid with his own pulsing release.

The feel of it inside her sent Roane over the edge again, leaving her limp as Adam collapsed on top of her, holding his weight on one elbow while they both struggled for breath.

'I'm sorry.' He mumbled the rough words into her hair. 'I'm so sorry.'

Roane felt her throat closing over at the shuddering breath he took after he said the words. She smoothed her hands over his back in circles, turned her head to kiss his throat. 'You have nothing to be sorry for.'

'I can't give you more than this.'

Roane choked out the words she wished with all her heart weren't true. 'You can't give me something that's not there. I know that.'

His head lifted and he looked down at her with the most tortured eyes she'd ever seen. 'It's not there. It never has been.'

She was still fighting the piercing agony of being told it wasn't there when she felt it so deeply for him when a sudden thought stole her breath away and twisted her battered heart. 'You don't think you can feel love?'

His gaze shifted to her hair as he brushed a strand of it off her heated cheek. 'I don't have it in me. That's what I've been telling you. That's why I'm sorry.'

'Who told you you couldn't?'

He shot her a brief frown. 'No one told me. I know. If I had it in me I'd have felt it by now. In case you hadn't noticed from what just happened—me and emotions? We don't get on so good.'

Roane blinked up at him in stunned amazement as he continued in a low, deep rumble that made it difficult for her to think. 'I get angry. A lot. It's better as I've got older 'cause I'm better at controlling it now, but being back here has reminded me of how it used to feel. Emotions are a variable—that's the problem. I like things with patterns and rhythms. Those I get.'

Somewhat miraculously it made complete sense to Roane. She'd been right—he did think entirely too much. He was the most intelligent man she'd ever known, he'd made a fortune from the fact he could figure out stocks and shares as easily as breathing in and out, but he hadn't a clue how to deal with emotions.

He looked into her eyes again. 'I can't lie to you. I've been economical with the truth the last few days but I can't lie. Not to you. Don't ask me why.'

Roane smiled at him, not caring if how she felt showed in her eyes. 'I know why.'

His brows lifted.

She wrapped her arms around him and lifted her chin. 'So the only reason you're not prepared to give this a try is because you think you're incapable of loving me, that's what you're saying?'

'That's what I'm saying. I want you, you know that. And I need you, God only knows how much. If I could feel more for anyone I'd feel it for you. But I can't.'

'Do you want to leave?'

It took a moment, then she got a low, 'No.'

'Do you want to see me with someone else?' His coarse answer made her flinch. 'That'd be a no then.'

'Damn right it would.' He frowned.

Moving a hand to frame his beautiful face, she brushed

her lips over his and asked, 'Do you want to make love with me every day and every night for the foreseeable future?'

The answering smile was so devilishly sexy it sent a shiver up her spine. 'Hell, yes.'

Smoothing her thumb back and forth against his cheek she continued smiling as she nodded. 'Me too.'

He studied her eyes for a long while. 'I'll still have to go at some point. You're saying you'll come with me, aren't you?'

'Yes. And you'll stay with me here too, won't you?'

'Yes. It might take a while to figure that out though…'

Roane's smile grew, the world suddenly brighter than it had ever been before. 'Yes, but it's a place to start. We could take it from there. See what happens. Consider me your fixed mark from the compass poem from here on in and I'll rely on you to make me soar on terra firma…'

'Now *that* I can do…' His smile faded a little.

But when he opened his mouth she set her finger over it to stop him, her voice soft with sincerity. 'Adam, I don't believe for a single second you're incapable of love. No one who makes love with the passion and the tenderness you do is incapable of love.' She tried to keep the smile on her face for the next part, but it wasn't easy. 'It might not be me you fall in love with. But I hope it is. I really do. Because…'

The words sat on the tip of her tongue, but when she saw the silent question in his sensational eyes she knew she wasn't going to stop them being said. No matter how soon it was or how far they had to go before she knew if she was having her heart broken…

She smiled tremulously. '*I* love *you*.'

Adam stared at her for what felt like for ever, then he moved his head enough to dislodge her thumb from her lips, his voice husky. 'You don't know me well enough to love me.'

She lifted her shoulders, her smile becoming shy. 'My heart says it knows you enough.'

His throat convulsed as he swallowed and Roane held her breath as she waited to see if he would argue with her or try and convince her she was wrong or laugh or—

'What does it feel like?' he asked.

Tears formed in her eyes. And just like that Roane knew they were going to be okay. They had time. And for as long as he wanted her they had a chance. One day at a time. She would love him with all her heart and pray every day that one day he'd feel the same about her.

She had to.

With a deep breath made difficult by the swell of her heart, she framed his face in both hands and nodded as she told him in a firmer voice, 'I still have a lot to teach you.'

Adam laughed. She loved it when he laughed. She loved him, period. Always would. End of story. If waiting for ever meant he'd love her one day, then she'd wait for him. He was worth it. And she had a sneaking suspicion a girl only got one naked Adonis on a beach per lifetime...

'We'll teach each other.'

'We will.'

Adam scooped her off the desk. 'I'm gonna teach you about joint showers now, sweetheart...so pay attention...'

EPILOGUE

Eighteen Months Later

THERE WERE CERTAIN days in a man's life, Adam decided, that stuck in his mind; a special day in a long chain of events. There was a pattern to that. He should have known if he looked hard he'd eventually find one.

The day he'd decided to go home, for example. That had been momentous. Life changing. More for the moment he'd got off his motorcycle dusty and sweaty and decided on impulse to take a swim in the ocean than for the trip itself. The first link in the chain…

Then there was the day he'd decided to make it plain she was going to end up in his bed. Okay, her bed. But it had been a bed. That was all that mattered. Another link in the chain…and he'd felt the same way she had regardless of the lie he'd told himself about her being a distraction—it was inevitable, was *right;* it made perfect sense when viewed with the rest of the chain.

The first time they'd made love would stay in his memory until the day he died. He didn't doubt that. Not just for how amazing it had been or how perfect or how seriously hot, but because he'd never wanted to see her cry like that again. That was the day she'd touched him in a way no other woman ever had—or ever would. Two links in the chain in one day. They'd maybe done things a little fast according to tradition—but then Adam had always been a bit of a rebel.

The next links—there were a ton of them all in the one day. But the one that had stuck most clearly in his mind now was when she'd said she would be his fixed mark. She was. No matter how many trips he took away from home or how many flights she made or how often they went to places together—she was a fixed mark in his life. A touchstone. A sounding board. A voice of reason when he wouldn't listen to anyone else. The one woman who could turn him on with a glance and soothe his soul with a touch…

Adam couldn't remember what his life had been like without her in it. He didn't want to. She loved him. She knew him better than anyone ever had and she said she loved him more each day. Yelled at him when she was mad; yes. But she loved how they'd make up…

The next day in the chain had been one neither of them had planned but they'd been overjoyed. Okay so Roane had been nervous about it at first but Adam had been ready to shout it from the hills. It had put a seal on the sense of everything somehow being meant to be. With time Adam's opinions on fairy tales like that were becoming more relaxed. Yes, she had that much influence over him.

He couldn't have said when he fell in love with Roane. But he knew the day he recognized it for what it was. And once he understood what it was he knew it had been there for a long time. Hints of it were scattered throughout, from the night she'd found him on the beach to the day he'd watched her walk across a crowded room to him and he'd just known—

he'd looked at her and she'd been everything there was to him. He'd known he would rather die than live without her.

So there, in the middle of the crowd, he'd framed her face with his hands and looked deep into her eyes so she knew he was telling the truth. He'd said the words for the first time.

'I love you.'

Her eyes had shimmered and she'd wrapped her arms around his waist. Then she'd simply lifted her mouth to his and told him in that soft voice of hers, 'I know you do. And I love you. I'll love you for ever.'

Adam was grateful for that every single day.

'So when are we getting hitched?' he'd teased her with a completely deadpan expression not long after.

'Oh, well, that's romantic—one for the grandkids right there. I can see their little eyes shining as Grandpa says the word "hitched" and everyone goes awww.' She shivered with mock delight and crinkled her nose before lifting her chin and cocking a brow at him the way only she could. 'Try again, Romeo. And when you get it right…I'll think about it.'

So he'd taken her to bed and made her say yes—again and again and again. Somehow he had a feeling the grandkids might get a watered-down version of the story.

Jake nudged his shoulder. 'She's here.'

Adam felt his breathing change, his heart swelling in his chest as he turned and watched her walking towards him. He knew he'd never forget how beautiful she was then, how calm and serene and *certain* that giving herself to him was right. How she looked straight into his eyes and smiled the smile that made him want to sweep her off her feet and carry her away…

He'd never got round to sating them both. He doubted very much he ever would.

Sunshine glinted off the pendant at the hollow of her neck:
her something old from the list—his wedding gift to her. It
had been passed back and forth for over a year, every time
one of them took a trip away from the other, but it was hers
now—the way she'd be his in a few minutes. But then she'd
always been his, hadn't she?

They even had their own quote. One that was as apt for
them as the one the compass had had before: 'I carry your
heart with me (I carry it in my heart).'—by E.E. Cummings.

Because he did—and she did—it was that simple.

Part of it was engraved inside the rings Jake had in his
pocket. Or had better have. He'd forgotten where he'd left the
box twice in the last week—hence the fidgeting he'd been
doing while they'd waited for her to make the walk onto the
beach.

Roane's fine-boned fingers tangled firmly with Adam's as
she stepped up beside him. Then she angled her head and hit
him with an impish smile, her voice low. 'You know this is
a private beach, right?'

'Ocean belongs to everyone, sweetheart.' He smiled back.
Man, but he loved her.

She mouthed she loved him too, then leaned around him
to ask, 'Got the rings, Jake?'

Adam dropped his chin and stifled a chuckle. But when
there wasn't an answer he pursed his lips, jerked his brows
at Roane and swung his head round to glare at his brother.
'You're kidding me, right?'

Jake held up the ring box with a grin.

'Loser,' Adam whispered.

'Jerk,' Jake whispered in reply.

Then Adam looked back at Roane and found her luminous
eyes dancing at him. So he winked and squeezed her fingers.

'Ready, woman?'

'More than ready.' She turned her head and smiled the most beautiful of smiles. 'Come on, honey. Your dad can hold you while we say the words.'

Adam released Roane just long enough to reach out large hands as two chubby arms stretched his way. 'Hello, little girl, remember me?'

That was the most memorable of his memorable days. He'd never forget the day he held their child for the first time. It'd been the most overwhelming thing he'd ever experienced. And for a man who'd once thought he was incapable of love, somewhat ironically he'd almost burst with how much of it he'd felt as he'd placed her in her mother's arms and looked at them both.

He'd even forgiven Roane's insistence she wouldn't marry him till she was pre-baby weight for a dress.

Yes, she'd taught him a lot, this woman of his. He planned on spending every day of the rest of his life thanking her for that. He loved her with all he was. And he didn't need to know how or why. Roane Elliott-soon-to-be-Bryant had taught him that too.

'Do you, Adam, take Roane…?'

Hell, yes, he'd take her. It had been her fantasy after all. And whatever made her happy…

* * * * *

*Celebrate 60 years of pure reading pleasure
with Harlequin®!*

*Harlequin Presents® is proud to introduce
its gripping new miniseries,*
THE ROYAL HOUSE OF KAREDES.
*An exquisite coronation diamond, split as a symbol of a
warring royal family's feud, is missing! But whoever
reunites the diamond halves will rule all....*

*Welcome to eight brand-new titles that unfold to reveal the
stories of kings and queens, princes and princesses torn
apart by pride and power, but finally reunited by love.*

Step into the world of Karedes with
BILLIONAIRE PRINCE, PREGNANT MISTRESS
*Available July 2009
from Harlequin Presents®.*

ALEXANDROS KAREDES, SNOW DUSTING the shoulders of his leather jacket and glittering like jewels in his dark hair, stood at the door. Maria felt the blood drain from her head.

"Good evening, Ms. Santos."

His voice was as she remembered it. Deep. Husky. Perfect English, but with the faintest hint of a Greek accent. And cold, as cold as it had been that awful morning she would never forget, when he'd accused her of horrible things, called her terrible names....

"Aren't you going to ask me in?"

She fought for composure. Last time they'd faced each other, they'd been on his turf. Now they were on hers. She was in command here, and that meant everything.

"There's a sign on the door downstairs," she said, her tone every bit as frigid as his. "It says, 'No soliciting or vagrants.'"

His lips drew back in a wolfish grin. "Very amusing."

"What do you want, Prince Alexandros?"

A tight smile eased across his mouth and it killed her that even now, knowing he was a vicious, arrogant man, she couldn't help but notice what a handsome mouth it was.

Chiseled. Generous. Beautiful, like the rest of him, which made him living proof that beauty could, indeed, be only skin deep.

"Such formality, Maria. You were hardly so proper the last time we were together."

She knew his choice of words was deliberate. She felt her face heat; she couldn't help that but she damned well didn't have to let him lure her into a verbal sparring match.

"I'll ask you once more, your highness. What do you want?"

"Ask me in and I'll tell you."

"I have no intention of asking you in. Tell me why you're here or don't. It's your choice, just as it will be my choice to shut the door in your face."

He laughed. It infuriated her but she could hardly blame him. He was tall—six two, six three—and though he stood with one shoulder leaning against the door frame, hands tucked casually into the pockets of the jacket, his pose was deceptive. He was strong, with the leanly muscled body of a well-trained athlete.

She remembered his body with painful clarity. The feel of him under her hands. The power of him moving over her. The taste of him on her tongue.

Suddenly, he straightened, his laughter gone. "I have not come this distance to stand in your doorway," he said coldly, "and I am not going to leave until I am ready to do so. I suggest you stand aside and stop behaving like a petulant child."

A petulant child? Was that what he thought? This man who had spent hours making love to her and had then accused her of—of trading her body for profit?

Except it had not been love, it had been sex. And the sooner she got rid of him, the better.

She let go of the doorknob and stepped aside. "You have five minutes."

He strolled past her, bringing cold air and the scent of the night with him. She swung toward him, arms folded. He reached past her, pushed the door closed, then folded his arms, too. She wanted to open the door again but she'd be damned if she was going to get into a who's-in-charge-here argument with him. She was in charge, and he would surely see a tussle over the ground rules as a sign of weakness.

Instead, she looked past him at the big clock above her work table.

"Ten seconds gone," she said briskly. "You're wasting time, your highness."

"What I have to say will take longer than five minutes."

"Then you'll just have to learn to economize. More than five minutes, I'll call the police."

Instantly, his hand was wrapped around her wrist. He tugged her toward him, his dark-chocolate eyes almost black with anger.

"You do that and I'll tell every tabloid shark I can contact about how Maria Santos tried to buy a five-hundred-thousand-dollar commission by seducing a prince." He smiled thinly. "They'll lap it up."

* * * * *

What will it take for this billionaire prince to realize
he's falling in love with his mistress…?
Look for
BILLIONAIRE PRINCE, PREGNANT MISTRESS
by Sandra Marton
Available July 2009 from Harlequin Presents®.

We'll be spotlighting a different series every month
throughout 2009 to celebrate our 60th anniversary.

Look for Harlequin® Presents in July!

TWO CROWNS, TWO ISLANDS, ONE LEGACY
A royal family, torn apart by pride and its lust for
power, reunited by purity and passion

Step into the world of Karedes
beginning this July with

BILLIONAIRE PRINCE,
PREGNANT MISTRESS
by
Sandra Marton

Eight volumes to collect and treasure!

FORCED TO MARRY

Wives for the taking!

Once these men put a diamond ring on their bride's
finger, there's no going back....

Wedlocked and willful, these wives will get a
wedding night they'll never forget!

**Read all the fantastic stories, out this month
in Harlequin Presents EXTRA:**

The Santangeli Marriage #61
by SARA CRAVEN

Salzano's Captive Bride #62
by DAPHNE CLAIR

The Ruthless Italian's
Inexperienced Wife #63
by CHRISTINA HOLLIS

Bought for Marriage #64
by MARGARET MAYO

HARLEQUIN *Presents*

International Billionaires

Life is a game of power and pleasure.
And these men play to win!

THE SHEIKH'S LOVE-CHILD
by *Kate Hewitt*

When Lucy arrives in the desert kingdom of Biryal,
Sheikh Khaled's eyes are blacker and harder than
before. But Lucy and the sheikh are inextricably
bound forever—for he is the father of her son....

Book #2838

Available July 2009

Two more titles to collect in this exciting miniseries:

**BLACKMAILED INTO THE GREEK
TYCOON'S BED** by *Carol Marinelli*
August

**THE VIRGIN SECRETARY'S
IMPOSSIBLE BOSS** by *Carole Mortimer*
September

HARLEQUIN *Presents*

TWO CROWNS, TWO ISLANDS, ONE LEGACY

A royal family, torn apart by pride and its lust for power, reunited by purity and passion

coming in 2009

BILLIONAIRE PRINCE, PREGNANT MISTRESS
by Sandra Marton, July

THE PLAYBOY SHEIKH'S VIRGIN STABLE-GIRL
by Sharon Kendrick, August

THE PRINCE'S CAPTIVE WIFE
by Marion Lennox, September

THE SHEIKH'S FORBIDDEN VIRGIN
by Kate Hewitt, October

THE GREEK BILLIONAIRE'S
INNOCENT PRINCESS
by Chantelle Shaw, November

THE FUTURE KING'S LOVE-CHILD
by Melanie Milburne, December

RUTHLESS BOSS, ROYAL MISTRESS
by Natalie Anderson, January

THE DESERT KING'S HOUSEKEEPER BRIDE
by Carol Marinelli, February

8 volumes to collect and treasure!

REQUEST YOUR FREE BOOKS!

2 FREE NOVELS PLUS 2 FREE GIFTS!

YES! Please send me 2 FREE Harlequin Presents® novels and my 2 FREE gifts (gifts are worth about $10). After receiving them, if I don't wish to receive any more books, I can return the shipping statement marked "cancel". If I don't cancel, I will receive 6 brand-new novels every month and be billed just $4.05 per book in the U.S. or $4.74 per book in Canada. That's a savings of close to 15% off the cover price! It's quite a bargain! Shipping and handling is just 25¢ per book*. I understand that accepting the 2 free books and gifts places me under no obligation to buy anything. I can always return a shipment and cancel at any time. Even if I never buy another book, the two free books and gifts are mine to keep forever.   106 HDN ERRW 306 HDN ERRL

Name _____ (PLEASE PRINT)

Address _____ Apt. #

City _____ State/Prov. _____ Zip/Postal Code

Signature (if under 18, a parent or guardian must sign)

Mail to the **Harlequin Reader Service:**
IN U.S.A.: P.O. Box 1867, Buffalo, NY 14240-1867
IN CANADA: P.O. Box 609, Fort Erie, Ontario L2A 5X3

Not valid to current subscribers of Harlequin Presents books.

Are you a current subscriber of Harlequin Presents books and want to receive the larger-print edition? Call 1-800-873-8635 today!

HP09

HARLEQUIN *Presents*

Undressed
BY THE BOSS

From sensible suits…into satin sheets!

Even if at times work is rather boring,
there is one person making the office
a whole lot more interesting: the boss!

SHEIKH BOSS, HOT DESERT NIGHTS
by Susan Stephens

Casey feels out of her depth around her new boss!
Sheikh Rafik al Rafar likes a challenge, and seduces
Casey in the sultry heat—in time to learn that Casey
can teach him some simpler pleasures in life….

Book #2842
Available July 2009

Look out for more of these supersexy titles
in this series!

www.eHarlequin.com

HP12842